## They were about halfway to the squad car when they heard the loud crack of a gunshot.

"Get down," Griff shouted, pushing Jenna and Claire to the ground and covering their bodies as much as possible with his.

"We need to get to the car," he whispered as he eased off them.

When they reached the relative safety of the squad car, Jenna pulled open the back passenger door, gesturing for Claire to get in first. "Keep your head down," she commanded.

There wasn't any sign of the shooter, although that didn't necessarily surprise Jenna. The shot had sounded as if it came from a rifle. No doubt the gunman was perched high on a tree branch or maybe on the roof of one of the houses across the street.

Jenna hated knowing that she'd somehow dragged Griff into this mess, right into the center of danger.

She glanced back at him. "I'm going to slide into the driver's seat. If they want Claire alive, he may confuse me for her and hold off on shooting," she said.

Jenna waited until Griff was safely inside before she hit the gas and pulled away from the curb. She held her breath as she drove, desperate to put distance between their car and the shooter.

**Laura Scott** is a nurse by day and an author by night. She has always loved romance, reading faith-based books by Grace Livingston Hill in her teenage years. She's thrilled to have published fifteen books for Love Inspired Suspense. She has two adult children and lives in Milwaukee, Wisconsin, with her husband of thirty years. Please visit Laura at laurascottbooks.com, as she loves to hear from her readers.

### Books by Laura Scott

### Love Inspired Suspense

*The Thanksgiving Target*
*Secret Agent Father*
*The Christmas Rescue*
*Lawman-in-Charge*
*Proof of Life*
*Identity Crisis*
*Twin Peril*
*Undercover Cowboy*
*Her Mistletoe Protector*

### SWAT: Top Cops

*Wrongly Accused*
*Down to the Wire*
*Under the Lawman's Protection*
*Forgotten Memories*
*Holiday on the Run*
*Mirror Image*

# MIRROR IMAGE

## LAURA SCOTT

**HARLEQUIN**® LOVE INSPIRED® SUSPENSE

Recycling programs
for this product may
not exist in your area.

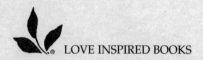

LOVE INSPIRED BOOKS

ISBN-13: 978-0-373-67744-3

Mirror Image

www.Harlequin.com

**Printed in U.S.A.**

This is the message we have heard from Him and declare to you: God is light; in Him there is no darkness at all.
*—1 John* 1:5

This book is dedicated to my Aunt Joan and Uncle Jerry Cook. Thanks for all the wonderful family memories!

# ONE

Sheriff's deputy Jenna Reed parked a few yards down the street from her house despite the late hour. She had a one-car garage in the alley, but the structure needed work, so she preferred parking on the street, as did most of her neighbors. As she darted around cars to make her way home, she frowned, slowing her pace when she noticed the front porch light wasn't on. Had she forgotten to flip the switch before leaving for work? Or had the bulb burned out? She thought she'd turned it on, but maybe not.

The cool spring breeze made her shiver, as she wore only a cotton blouse and denim jacket. She and her teammates had celebrated her colleague Caleb O'Malley's promotion after work at Joey's Pizzeria. They'd all changed out of their uniforms for the party, which was a good thing since their boss, Griff Vaughn, had unexpectedly joined them. Seeing off-duty officers in uniform was just one of their lieutenant's pet peeves.

Jenna was cutting across the lawn, heading toward her front porch, when she sensed someone behind her. She whirled, but a second too late. Large hands roughly grabbed her from behind, nearly jerking her off her feet.

Jenna's reaction was swift. Kicking back with her booted foot, she caught her assailant's kneecap with her heel. The hands loosened momentarily but then tightened, an arm sliding around her neck, cutting off her airway. The scent of stale cigar smoke clung to her captor's clothing. She refused to panic, instead using her elbows and heels to fight back while attempting to pry the muscular arm from around her neck.

For what seemed like endless minutes, she struggled with the man who'd grabbed her, her heart beating frantically in her chest as she fought for air. She hated feeling weak, and for a moment the attack reminded her of the night she'd had to fight her father.

*No!*

Jenna kicked back again at her assailant's knees, and her booted heel found its mark. The arm loosened around her neck enough that she could get her hands up to break out of the hold. Then she spun in a roundhouse kick, catching her attacker in the solar plexus.

He staggered backward but didn't fall down. Jenna wasted precious seconds debating whether or not she could outrun him, but he was already moving deliberately toward her again.

She dropped into a fighting stance, keeping her eyes on the assailant, who wore a black ski mask covering his face. She'd been in tough situations before, but nothing quite like this. She had no idea why this guy had targeted her, and he outweighed her by at least a hundred pounds.

He lashed out with his fist, connecting with her jaw despite her attempt to duck out of the way. Pain exploded in her face, but she ignored it, taking a step back.

*Block with your forearm!*

Lessons learned during her police-academy training echoed in her mind as she kept her distance from her attacker. She'd survived being attacked by her father all those years ago; certainly she could survive this.

*Lord, give me strength!*

His fist came out again, and this time she brought her arm up in time to prevent the blow from landing. Pain radiated up her arm, but she quickly lashed out with her other fist, aiming for his nose. Her aim was low and she hit his mouth instead, his teeth scraping the skin off her knuckles.

They fought in a blur of motion, time seeming to stand still. Just when Jenna thought she'd beaten him, he sent her flying backward to land hard on the concrete sidewalk.

She tried to suck air into her lungs, even as he continued toward her like a lion stalking his prey. Jenna couldn't bear the thought of allowing this guy to get the better of her, so she struck out once again with her foot, kicking him in the groin.

He bent over, muttering a curse as she attempted to scramble to her feet. But then he straightened and reached for her. "I've got you now," he said in a low tone.

"Stop! Police!"

Jenna was just as surprised as her attacker when the harsh voice cut through the silence of the night.

Her assailant spun around and disappeared before Jenna could regain her footing. She sensed someone running toward her, but she didn't wait for the officer to catch up. She managed to scramble upright and took off after the thug. When she reached the edge of her house, she paused, staring through the darkness, uncertain where he might have gone.

There was no sign of him.

She leaned against the tan brick wall for a moment, trying to calm her racing heart, inwardly berating herself for letting him get away.

What kind of SWAT cop was she? If this had happened to Nate Freemont, or one of the other officers, they'd no doubt have been able to take down and capture the guy without a problem.

Then again, she had managed to hold her own.

No easy task when her opponent was taller, more muscular and had the advantage of catching her off guard. Which was her fault, as well, she acknowledged with a sigh. Jenna straightened her shoulders and turned to face the officer who'd come rushing to her rescue.

But her brief moment of relief sank to the soles of her feet when she recognized her lieutenant, Griffin Vaughn, jogging toward her, his expression etched in what she suspected was a permanent scowl.

He was the last guy on the entire planet she wanted or expected to see. Especially in a moment of weakness. But she pulled herself together with an effort and lifted her aching chin, determined to show her boss that she was a cop first and foremost.

She'd never be a victim again.

Griff couldn't believe the brutal attack on Jenna he'd stumbled across when he'd driven down her street.

*Deputy Reed*, he reminded himself firmly, as he closed the distance between them.

"Are you all right?" he asked, his voice coming out more harshly than he'd intended. He raked his gaze over her, trying to assure himself that she wasn't harmed.

"Yeah, I'm fine. What are you doing here, Lieutenant?"

Griff inwardly sighed, wishing she'd call him Griff the way the rest of his deputies did. She was the only one who continued to use his title, and for some reason that fact grated on him. "You left your credit card at Joey's, and since I was on my way back to work, I volunteered to drop it off." He held out the plastic card, glad he'd left the pizzeria when he did. The thought of not getting here in time made him feel sick to his stomach. "Who was that guy? Did you recognize him?"

She tucked the card into her back pocket, then shook her head, lifting her hand to massage her shoulder as if it hurt. "He wore a ski mask and didn't say much, so unfortunately not."

Griff hated the thought of Jenna being injured and forced himself to glance around her front yard, trying to figure out what had happened. "No demand to hand over money?" When she shook her head, he scowled. "Seems strange. Why else would he attack you? Maybe you should get inside. I'll call for backup."

Jenna frowned and planted her hands on her hips. "I don't need to go inside. Call this in if you want, but I'm going to go around back to make sure he's not hanging out somewhere nearby."

Griff hid a wince, knowing she had a right to be upset. After all, he'd hired her. He knew she was a capable deputy on the SWAT team. She was an ace sharpshooter and could handle herself.

So why the need to protect her? Because

he still wrestled with guilt over his role in his wife's death?

He shied away from that thought. "We'll both sweep the area," he amended. "You go left. I'll go right. If we don't find anything, no need to call for reinforcements."

Jenna gave a curt nod. "Give me a minute to grab my weapon."

He waited while she opened her front door, collected her service weapon and came back outside. He wished she'd still been in uniform, because he was certain the assailant wouldn't have got away so easily if she'd had her gun. His fault that she wasn't. He knew all the deputies had changed because of his penchant for following the rules.

Griff watched her disappear into the shadows before heading in the opposite direction.

He tightened his grip on his .38, moving slowly across Jenna's front yard to the north side of the house. There were plenty of trees on the neighbor's lawn, and he peered through the darkness, trying to see if anyone was hiding there.

He moved from the edge of the house to the closest tree. Nothing seemed out of place and he was a little surprised that the fight between Jenna and her assailant hadn't garnered more attention from the neighbors. Granted, it was late, but surely someone would have heard something and come out to investigate.

The faint sound of a car starting caught his attention, and he recognized the unique clicking associated with a diesel engine.

Did the perp have a getaway car hidden nearby? If that was the case, he'd be long gone. Griff squinted, trying to make out any sign of a car in the darkness. He couldn't see anything, not even headlights.

After making sure no one was lingering behind the neighbor's trees or shrubs, he made his way into Jenna's backyard. There was a nice little patio with a round table, four chairs and a decent-sized grill.

He could easily imagine Jenna sitting outside, enjoying her patio while grilling burgers and brats. Not too different from the life he'd once envisioned for himself and Helen.

Griff closed off the painful reminders of his past to focus on the here and now. He crossed over to meet Jenna, who was coming in from the other side.

"No sign of him," she said with obvious disgust. "No doubt you scared him off."

"Probably. Or he had a car parked nearby." Up close, he could see that she was bleeding from the corner of her lip, and the edge of her jaw was beginning to swell. "Let's get some ice for your chin."

She grimaced and gingerly palpated the tender area. "Yeah, he packed a mean punch."

Griff took her arm to escort her to the front of the house. He swept a keen eye over the area as she opened the door, flipped on the lights and crossed the threshold.

He followed her into the kitchen and then hesitated in the doorway as she rummaged in the freezer for a bag of frozen peas. The corner of his mouth kicked up in a smile. What would she say if she knew his cold pack of choice was a bag of frozen corn?

"Much better," she mumbled, pressing the bag against her jaw.

His smile instantly evaporated when he noticed the dark bruise marring her beautiful skin. "Are you sure you don't know him?" he pressed. "Maybe an old boyfriend?"

She rolled her eyes in a flash of annoyance. "I only have one old boyfriend, and we broke up six months ago," she said, moving the bag of frozen peas so she could talk. "Eric used words as a weapon, not his fists, and he wasn't as tall or broad in the shoulders. I was thinking more along the lines of this guy being a part of some case I worked on. Or maybe someone connected to the women's shelter I help support. You know as well as I do, this isn't the kind of job where we make many friends."

He stared at Jenna for a moment, not liking the thought of her ex-boyfriend using words to lash out at her. Obviously, she was better off without him.

She was younger than Griff by almost five years, had long blond hair, bright blue eyes and a lean frame that was toned without being overly muscular. Her light blue blouse and denim jacket complemented her eyes.

Not that he should notice just how attractive she was. He wasn't at all interested in going down the path of having a relationship. Not after the way he'd lost his wife just two years ago.

Two years, but at times it seemed like yesterday.

"Put the ice back on your jaw," he said mildly. Once she did as he requested, he returned to the mysterious assailant. "Okay, so maybe you're right about this guy being connected to one of your cases. Anyone in particular stand out in your mind? Anyone at the shelter have an angry ex?"

She shrugged. "All of the women at the shelter have angry exes or they wouldn't be there. But no one specific comes to mind. And nothing stands out in any of my recent cases, either."

He'd been afraid she'd say that. After all, they'd worked dozens of cases over the past year. And Jenna was well-known in the community as an advocate for abused women, too. "Fine. Then we should go through the recent ones and see who might have gotten released from jail."

She arched an eyebrow. "For all we know, the perp could be related to someone in jail. Or was paid to attack me."

He didn't want to think about the endless possibilities. "You could be right, but somehow I get the sense that this was personal."

She stared at him curiously. "Why do you think that?"

He was caught off guard by the fact that he wanted to go and gently hold the ice pack against the bruise himself. What was wrong with him? It wasn't the first time one of his deputies had got injured. Just a few months ago, Deputy Nate Freemont had been shot in the line of duty.

He cared about the deputies who reported to him. But, for some reason, he found himself more preoccupied with Jenna's attack and subsequent injury than he should be.

The image of the guy slugging Jenna hard enough to send her sprawling backward onto the hard, unforgiving concrete was etched in his memory. The vicious attack had come out of nowhere. There had to be some reason for it.

When he realized she was waiting for him to answer, he shrugged. "He didn't use a knife or gun, which is what most assailants would use to get what they want. Not to mention he didn't ask for money. And he hit you directly in the face, which is always an indication of being personally involved with the victim."

She nodded slowly. "You're right. We learned about that at the academy."

"Tell me how he approached you," Griff continued. "Did he call you by name? Or just grab you?"

"He didn't call me by name, but he did grab me from behind," she admitted. "He locked his arm across my throat so I couldn't breathe. He smelled like stale cigar smoke."

It was too easy to visualize exactly what had happened. He frowned with concern. "How did you get away?"

She sent him an exasperated look. "I did pass self-defense training, you know. I finally caught him a good one in the kneecap, enough at least to make him loosen his grip. That was all I needed to break away from him."

"Then what happened?"

"He kept coming after me," she said in a matter-of-fact tone.

Griff swallowed hard, wondering what the assailant had intended. A physical beating? Or worse, a sexual assault?

Neither option was at all acceptable.

"Do you have time to go and look through old files now?" he asked, driven by the need to find out just who this guy was. The sooner they had a suspect, the sooner they could slap cuffs on him and drag him into custody. "We can also review the known assailants of women who you've recently taken to the shelter, see if anyone looks at all familiar."

She hesitated, then shrugged. "Sure. Why not? I probably won't get much sleep anyway."

He caught a glimpse of the open scratches on her hand. "Wait a minute. What did those come from?"

She glanced down at her hand and smirked. "I managed to catch him in the mouth with my fist. Too bad—I was aiming for his nose."

Griff almost smiled at her wry sense of humor. Jenna was tough; he knew that better than anyone. But it still bothered him to see her get hurt. "That settles it. We need to go to the hospital, see if there's any DNA evidence we can use."

She nodded, adjusting the frozen peas against her jaw. "You're right. It's worth a shot."

"Wrap your hand in a brown paper bag to preserve the evidence, and I'll drive you to the hospital," he said, glad to take some sort of action. He was determined to find this jerk, no matter what it took.

"Okay, okay, give me a sec." She turned and set down the peas to rifle through a junk drawer, finally coming up with a badly wrinkled brown lunch bag and a roll of tape. She stuck her hand inside the bag and awkwardly wrapped the tape around her wrist to hold the bag in place. Then she grabbed her makeshift ice pack with her free hand. "Okay, I'm ready."

He nodded and stepped to the side so she could precede him out of the kitchen. He followed her to the front door, where she stopped abruptly.

"Hang on a sec," she said, removing the frozen peas from her jaw to reach out for the light switch. She flipped one lever on and off several times, then pushed past him to head outside.

"What's wrong?" he asked when she craned her neck in an attempt to see something overhead.

"I need to see inside the light fixture." She glanced back at him. "Aim the screen of your phone up there."

He did as she asked, as understanding dawned. "Something wrong with the light?"

"I noticed my porch light was out when I drove up," she confessed. "Looks as if someone removed the lightbulb."

It took a minute for her statement to sink into his brain. "You mean on purpose?"

She nodded slowly. "Yeah. I guess you were right. This obviously wasn't a random event. This was a premeditated, personal attack."

The hint of fear in her blue eyes stabbed deep. This was one time he wished his instincts hadn't been right.

Maybe they'd catch a break with the DNA, but he wasn't banking on it. The real problem would be trying to find a way to keep Jenna safe while she continued to do her job as a SWAT team member.

An impossible task, at best.

"Wait a minute. What's that?" Jenna asked with a frown. She bent down next to the porch, tucking the peas under her arm so she could lift something out of the dirt. She stood and held up what looked to be a shiny bracelet.

"Is that yours?" he asked, when she simply stared at it with a troubled expression in her eyes.

"Shine your phone on it," she said in a hoarse tone.

He did as she asked. She peered at the item of jewelry. From what he could tell, it was a silver chain with a small heart-shaped charm dangling from it.

"That's odd," Jenna muttered.

A warning tingle skated down his spine. "What's odd?"

"This looks like mine, but it's not."

"Well, maybe it belongs to a neighbor?" Griff wasn't sure why she was so unnerved about a piece of jewelry. "Some kids might have been running around the neighborhood and accidentally dropped it."

"No, you don't understand. The letter *C* is engraved on the heart, see?" She lifted her head to look at him. "I have the exact same bracelet with the letter *J* engraved on the heart-shaped charm. It was a gift from my mother."

The warning tingle became a full-fledged wave of apprehension. He couldn't help turning and sweeping a cautious gaze around her front yard, searching for anything else out of the ordinary.

After being a cop for the past ten years, he didn't much believe in coincidences.

His instincts were screaming at him that this bracelet was somehow connected to the mysterious attack on Jenna.

# TWO

As Griff drove to the hospital, Jenna stared at the bracelet that he'd tucked into a clear plastic bag. Weird that it was identical to hers in every way, except for the engraved initial.

Offhand, she couldn't think of anyone who lived nearby whose first name started with a *C*.

There was no reason to believe the bracelet was an indication of something sinister. It didn't look especially unique or rare. There were likely dozens sold every month. Every year. But she couldn't seem to shake off the prickle of warning that danced along her nape.

Was the attack connected to it? And if so, how? Why?

There were no answers, so she tucked the bracelet into the front pocket of her jeans and tried to shake off the remnants of the attack. Glancing at Griff, she tried to think of something to say. Idle chitchat wasn't something that came naturally to her.

And apparently not to Griff, either, as he made no attempt to break the strained silence stretching endlessly between them. Everything seemed way more awkward than normal because he was her boss.

She forced herself to look away from his ruggedly attractive features and tried to think back over her most recent cases. There were literally dozens of them, but most of the criminals they'd apprehended were small-time crooks. For several long seconds, she'd assumed the attacker was her father, since he'd just been released from prison and was out on parole. But the guy who'd grabbed her was much larger than her father. She had the sense he was younger, too, although that was just a fleeting impression.

No, the attack had to be related to her work, either on the SWAT team or through the shelter. In the past month she'd helped Shelia and Janet get away from their exes by driving them personally to Ruth's shelter. There was one major drug ring that she'd assisted her colleague Nate Freemont with right before Christmas. Was it possible this attack was related to that in some way?

She glanced over at Griff's chiseled profile, wondering if she dared broach the possibility. Griff hadn't been very happy with her—or with Nate, for that matter—because they hadn't come to him at the first sign of trouble. Nate, in particular, had gone off on his own, determined to protect an innocent woman and her daughter. Because she'd agreed to help Nate and Melissa get the evidence they needed to expose a murderer, Griff had reamed Jenna out, too.

And placed a formal reprimand in her file.

She was tempted to keep her theories about the connection to Nate's case to herself, but since Nate was out of town with his fiancée, Melissa, and still on medical leave, she wasn't sure who else she could confide in.

She'd never told Griff that Melissa and her daughter had reminded her of the women and children who lived in fear at the shelter. She knew there were rumors among her coworkers about why she cared about the shelter so much, but she didn't bother to comment on them. Her past wasn't any of their business.

Griff's, either. As far as she was concerned, none of the guys she worked with needed to know how she spent her free time.

The hospital wasn't far, and soon the impressive building loomed before them. Griff parked the car and glanced over at her. "Ready?"

"Sure." She pushed open the door with her left hand and slid out of the seat.

"Hopefully we'll be in and out quickly," Griff said. "We need time to review mug shots."

She didn't think reviewing photographs of suspects would help, but arguing with her boss wasn't exactly an option. "I was thinking that maybe this attack is related to the Brookmont case," she offered, as Griff held the door open for her. "If you remember, I'm the one who took down the crooked police chief, Randall Joseph, the night Nate was shot. Maybe he's carrying a grudge."

Griff's dark eyes pierced hers. "Good point." He surprised her by agreeing. "You and Nate broke open the drug-trafficking ring and solved a twelve-year-old murder. Although I'm sure the former police chief is still in prison awaiting trial."

"I know, but it wouldn't take much for him to hire someone to come after me," she pointed out. "And if that's true, then Nate is in just as much danger."

Griff's reply was little more than a grunt as he walked with her up to the triage desk. She could see the nurse's eyes widen with interest as she took in Griff's short blond hair, dark brown eyes and broad shoulders. For a moment Jenna had to squelch a flash of jealousy, which was ridiculous. She didn't want to date her boss, or anyone else she worked with, for that matter. In her opinion, the other deputies on her team didn't always take her seriously now, and it would be ten times worse if she actually went out with one of them.

Which was part of the reason she'd thought Eric Krause was a good choice. They'd met at a fund-raiser for abused women and children, and she had thought they shared the same ideas and morals.

She'd never anticipated his verbal abuse and pathological need for control, and she had broken things off the night he'd shouted at her about how stupid she was. There had been a brief moment when she'd had a flashback to her father screaming the same words at her mother.

Thankfully, she hadn't dated Eric very long and none of her coworkers had known about him. Most of her fellow deputies already had women in their lives. Well, except the new guy who'd replaced Aaron Simms. She couldn't deny she'd been happy to see Simms leave the team. He'd been a challenge to work with.

And she hadn't told anyone the truth about what had transpired between them. How much he'd hated knowing she could outshoot him. One night, he'd shown up unexpectedly at her house after work. She'd been fortunate to get away when he'd tried to prove how much of a man he was. She'd threatened to file sexual-harassment charges against him, and thankfully, he'd decided to resign instead.

As much as it made sense that Simms might want to attack her, the build of the guy who'd grabbed her had seemed to be much bigger.

Jenna swept a glance over the waiting room, noting with dismay that every available seat was taken. Despite her lieutenant's plan to be in and out quickly, she suspected there would be a long wait time. No way did she want to sit here all night.

"Maybe we should wake up one of the crime-scene techs to swab my hand," she said to Griff. "This place is packed and we'll end up waiting forever."

Griff didn't even look at her, his gaze focused on the triage nurse who was practically drooling over him. "Excuse me. Is Dr. Gabriella Hawkins working tonight?" he asked.

The smile on the nurse's face faded a bit as she clearly wondered if his interest in Gabby was personal. Which was crazy, since Gabby had recently married Deputy Shane Hawkins and the two of them were giddy with happiness. "Yes, actually, Dr. Hawkins is on call tonight."

"Will you page her for us? We just need five minutes of her time." Griff's stern expression softened when he smiled at the nurse. She nodded and quickly accessed the computer to respond to his request.

Jenna sucked in a breath and turned away to stare blindly at the patrons in the waiting room. She couldn't remember the last time she'd seen Griff smile, and the simple gesture changed his entire face, making him even more attractive.

She gave herself a mental shake. She needed to get over herself already. Maybe it was a good thing Griff had never smiled at her like that. She was sure she'd babble like an imbecile if he did.

"I hope Gabby's not in the middle of surgery or something else equally important," Griff said in an undertone. "I'd like to get out of here before sunrise."

His dry tone made her smile. "Yeah, no kidding. This place is crazy busy."

For a moment their gazes clashed and clung, the space between them sizzling with awareness. Jenna felt powerless to break the bizarre connection, so she was grateful Gabby chose that moment to arrive and interrupt them.

"Hi, Lieutenant. Jenna. Is something wrong?"

Jenna found the strength to look away from Griff and acknowledge Gabby. "Hey, Doc, how are you?" She strove for a carefree tone, when in reality she felt anything but.

She seriously needed distance from Griff. Now.

"I'm fine, but what on earth happened to you?" Gabby reached out to lightly touch Jenna's aching jaw. "This must hurt."

"Nothing major, just a little run-in with one of the bad guys," Jenna replied, sneaking a glance at Griff's stone face. What was wrong with him? Had he felt the weird attraction that flashed between them, too? No, most likely it was just her overactive imagination working against her. She smiled at Gabby and lifted her hand, still wrapped in the brown paper lunch bag. "We need some evidence and hoped you would sneak us in to get my wounds swabbed."

"Absolutely. This way," Gabby said, gesturing for them to follow her through some double doors leading back into the emergency department. "We can use a room in the minor-care area."

Jenna nodded and followed Gabby into a small exam room. "I caught the perp in the mouth," she explained as she carefully removed the paper bag. "We're hoping to get saliva for DNA evidence."

"Understood," Gabby said, pulling supplies out of the cabinet located in the corner of the room. "When I'm finished, I'll wash the wounds out for you, too."

Jenna grimaced. "I can wash my own hands," she said, feeling as if the doc was making way too big a deal out of a few scratches that she barely felt compared to her jaw, which continued to throb painfully.

"Thanks. We'd appreciate that," Griff interjected as if she hadn't spoken. "The human mouth is full of germs."

Jenna tried not to roll her eyes at his comment. Griff had hired her almost two years ago and she wanted to believe that he'd made that decision based on her abilities. But sometimes she couldn't help wondering if she was nothing more than the token female.

Would she ever be taken seriously as a cop? Granted, the guys on the team knew she could shoot, but as far as other tactical situations were concerned, she often felt as if her teammates were trying to protect her.

She sighed and took a seat on the edge of the examining table, waiting patiently as Gabby pulled out the necessary supplies. Swabbing her wounds didn't take long, and when Gabby had finished, Jenna quickly jumped down to her feet, crossed over to the sink in the room and thrust her hands beneath the stream of water. The antibacterial soap stung on her open cuts, but she ignored the pain while making sure she thoroughly cleansed the wounds.

Getting an infection would only make things worse.

She could tell Griff wasn't happy, but he didn't push the issue, either.

"I have a colleague who works at the state lab in Madison," Gabby said. "I'll ask him to put a rush on this for you."

"Great—thanks for your help," Griff said, as Gabby finished labeling the swab samples. "I owe you one."

"No problem." Gabby's gaze was curious when she glanced at Jenna. "How's your head?

Maybe we should take an X-ray, make sure nothing is broken."

"I'm fine," Jenna insisted in a curt tone. "Trust me, I've been hit much harder than this." She turned toward Griff. "Are you ready to get out of here?"

Griff's fierce scowl didn't faze her in the least. She didn't care if he was all tough and growly. He was being ridiculous, and he must have realized that, too, because he finally nodded. "Yeah. Thanks again, Doc," he said.

"Anytime, Lieutenant."

Jenna walked out of the ER and headed straight outside, wishing she'd brought her own set of wheels. Griff easily kept pace with her, reaching out to open the passenger-side door for her before she could do it herself.

The gesture was polite, but she couldn't help spinning around to glare at him. "What is up with you, Lieutenant?" she demanded querulously.

Griff raised his eyebrows, obviously caught off guard by her uncharacteristic spurt of anger. "What are you talking about?"

"This," she said, waving an impatient hand toward the passenger-side door. "As if you'd do this for Nate, Deck or Isaac."

The corner of Griff's mouth twitched as if he found her amusing. "Hate to point this out, Reed, but you're not Nate, Deck, Isaac or any of the other male deputies who report to me. Now, will you please stop making a big deal out of nothing and get in? We still need to review those mug shots."

She bit back another retort, knowing she'd only make things worse if she continued to harp on his chivalrous behavior. She slid into the car and buckled the seat belt as she waited for Griff to get in behind the wheel.

To be honest, she shouldn't take her bad mood out on Griff. Being attacked and then finding the bracelet, so much like her own, had put her on edge. In addition, Griff's innocent act of opening her door had reminded her of Eric. Eric had seemed like such a nice guy at first, polite, charming. A facade that hadn't lasted long.

She didn't know Griff very well, and that was just fine with her, since she obviously couldn't rely on her instincts when it came to relationships. She knew better than most that men were not to be trusted. Even cops, like Aaron Simms. Far better to keep her distance from the lieutenant. As soon as they'd looked at mug shots, they'd go their separate ways.

Besides, she needed to focus on getting her life back on track. On helping the women at the shelter. On making sure her father didn't violate the no-contact order that was still in place.

But the first thing on her list was to investigate the bracelet she'd found near her doorstep.

* * *

Griff could feel the tension radiating off Jenna in waves. He tightened his grip on the steering wheel and tried to stay focused, even though the strawberry scent of her shampoo permeated the inside of his SUV.

They were going to look at mug shots. Nothing more. Jenna was a deputy who reported to him. Off-limits in more ways than he could count. Besides, he wasn't interested in a relationship, not after the way he'd indirectly caused his wife's death. Granted, he wasn't the one who'd run a red light, but he had been driving.

He'd supported his wife through law school and had been proud of her when she'd obtained a position at a high-powered law firm doing corporate legal work and family law. Helen had been passionate about her career but innocent in some ways to the seedy side of life. Jenna was tough, edgy, and had a chip on her shoulder the size of Mount Hood. Okay, maybe Jenna had a point about the way he'd instinctively opened doors for her, but she was a woman. His grandmother had ingrained manners into him from the moment he'd gone to live with her at the tender age of eight, after his parents were killed.

When Griff had learned the details of how his parents had operated on the wrong side of the law, he'd made a silent promise to be a cop. To bring people like his parents to justice.

He blew out his breath and concentrated on getting back to the issue at hand. One of his deputies had been brutally assaulted, and he was determined to find out who was holding a grudge against Jenna and why. And how did the bracelet fit in, if at all?

She had a point about the Brookmont scandal. The arrests of the crooked mayor and police chief had rocked the foundation of the entire city. Especially once they'd uncovered the drug running that had been going on for several years right beneath the public's nose.

"You really think this recent attack on you is related to Brookmont's former chief of police?" he asked, breaking the silence.

"I think it's a possibility we can't afford to ignore," she said. "It's a good thing that Nate happens to be down in South Carolina helping to move Melissa's stuff back here. Maybe he should extend his leave of absence a bit. If they're coming after me, they'd likely go after him, too."

"True," Griff agreed. He slanted a glance at Jenna. "And you're sure no one is giving you a hard time? What about the new guy, Jake Matthews?"

"He's fine," she said with a careless shrug. "Seems to fit in well enough. Better than Simms ever did."

He lifted a brow at the bitter note. He'd known there was tension between Jenna and Simms, but it was possible that more had transpired between the two of them than he realized. Had Simms made a move on her? Griff clenched his jaw and reminded himself that he preferred to have his deputies handle their interpersonal issues on their own.

Logic that didn't work well when it came to Jenna.

He turned into the parking lot of the building that housed his office and parked near the entrance. He climbed out from behind the wheel and met Jenna at the door. After unlocking it, he held it open so she could precede him inside.

Jenna led the way to his office and dropped into a chair as he took his familiar seat behind the desk. He booted up his computer and clicked on the file that contained their closed cases.

"Here. Do any of these guys seem like they may have been the one who attacked you?" he asked, turning his computer screen toward her so she could see the faces of their most recent arrests.

She pinched the bridge of her nose, frowning as she peered intently at the mug shots. Each time she shook her head, he flipped to the next page.

After about fifteen photos, she sat back with a sigh. "The last one, Corey Rock, has a similar height and muscular build," she admitted. "But I don't see why he'd have a personal grudge against me. If I remember correctly, Isaac was the one who arrested him. I was the spotter up on the building across the street."

"I'm sure he saw you at trial," Griff felt compelled to point out. "After all, you were one of the witnesses to his little shooting spree."

"Yeah, but it still seems out of proportion for him to come after me like that. The guy who grabbed me clearly wanted to physically take me down, as if to punish me. I have to agree with you that it's odd he didn't try to use a weapon."

Griff nodded, then reached over to shut down the computer. "Okay, let's call it a night. I'll drop you off at home."

For a minute it looked as if she wanted to protest, but she gave in with a brief nod. "Fine. Tomorrow morning I'll see if I can find any link to the Brookmont matter. The more I think about it, the more I believe that the guy who attacked me might have been sent by the former police chief. You'll warn Nate?"

Griff couldn't deny that taking down a huge drug ring placed both Nate and Jenna at risk for revenge. "Yeah, I'll call him. And I expect you to let me know if you find anything. I'll see if there's anything I can shake loose from the DA's office. Maybe they have a list of Randall Joseph's known associates."

"Sounds good." Jenna turned and walked out of the office. He followed close on her heels.

This time, when Jenna approached the SUV, he held back from opening the door for her. She lifted a brow and smiled, as if reading his thoughts.

The ride to Jenna's house didn't take long, and when he pulled onto her street he found an empty parking spot near the front of her house. When he stopped the car, he noticed she already had her hand on the door latch, ready to bolt.

He put out a hand to stop her, concerned that the assailant might have returned in their absence. And when he caught a flash of movement near the corner of her house, he knew his instincts were right on.

"Wait—I think there's someone out there," he said in a hushed tone.

"Where?" Jenna whispered, pressing her face to the window.

"Near your house." He stared through the darkness, wondering if he'd let his imagination get the better of him.

"I don't see anything," she said after several long minutes. "I'll be fine. This time, I have my gun."

Tough to argue that logic. He dropped his hand and watched helplessly as she pushed open the passenger-side door.

"Later, Lieutenant," she said before closing the door with a solid thud.

Griff didn't move from his spot on the street,

even after Jenna opened her door and disappeared inside.

He reminded himself she was a highly trained deputy on their SWAT team.

He waited five minutes. Then ten. Just as he was about to drive away, he caught another glimpse of movement.

Enough to have him turning off the car and charging out of the vehicle to make sure the assailant hadn't returned to finish what he'd started.

# THREE

Jenna pulled the bracelet out of her pocket as she headed into her bedroom to find the small jewelry box she had stashed in the top drawer of her dresser. She opened the lid, gently lifted her bracelet out and set it beside the one still contained in the plastic bag.

They were identical in size, shape and every other detail, except for the engraved initial on the heart-shaped charm. If her mother was still alive, Jenna would have called to ask where the bracelet had been purchased. But Jenna had lost her shortly after graduating from the police academy.

It wasn't likely her father would know anything about it, either. Besides, he was the last person on earth she wanted to talk to. It still burned to know he'd done only ten years of his twenty-year sentence for attempting to murder Jenna and her mother.

After his arrest, Ruth's shelter had been their

home for several months while the slow wheels of justice slogged forward on her father's case. Only once he was found guilty were she and her mom able to come out of hiding. They moved in with Grandpa Hank, her maternal grandfather, managing to scrape by on her mother's waitressing tips from the nearby café.

When Jenna was old enough to work, she joined her mother as a waitress. But she'd always known that she wanted to be a cop.

Just like the female officer who'd come to their rescue on that fateful night.

She shook off the disturbing memories and carried the bracelets into the living room, where she'd left her laptop. The hour was edging toward two in the morning, but she knew she wouldn't sleep until she'd at least tried to find some information on the bracelet.

She'd just clicked on a search engine when she heard a muffled thud from somewhere outside. She rose to her feet and reached for her weapon. Then she quickly doused the lights and inched toward the living room window, which overlooked the street.

She frowned when she noticed Griff's squad car was still parked at the curb. But why? She squinted, trying to see if he was inside.

Then she realized he was running toward the south side of her house as if he was going after someone.

The attacker was back!

Jenna didn't waste any time, but quickly opened the front door and headed outside. When she saw Griff disappearing around the corner, she took off after him.

She was light on her feet, gaining on Griff as he veered around the trees in her neighbor's yard. She couldn't see who he was chasing, but the least she could do was back him up.

As she closed the gap between them, he slowed, obviously hearing her behind him.

"Reed on your six," she whispered.

He didn't hesitate, but nodded, indicating he'd heard.

She put on a burst of speed so that she could run alongside him. "Who are you following?"

He glared at her for a moment, looking annoyed. "A teenage girl was hiding around the corner of your house."

A teenage girl? That didn't make any sense. But there wasn't time to argue as Griff veered around some lawn furniture, making her realize he had a destination in mind.

He slowed down, gesturing for her to come closer. He leaned in, his mouth next to her ear. "Behind the tan shed ahead. We'll need to circle around to meet in the back."

She gave a terse nod, then ducked around a low branch of a huge maple tree. She couldn't begin to fathom why a teenager would be hanging around her house, but the timing was certainly suspicious. Being in law enforcement had proved to her that anything was possible, so right now they were approaching this suspect carefully. It was entirely possible this girl was somehow connected to the earlier assault.

Stepping carefully, Jenna approached the edge of the shed. Leaning against the wooden structure, she listened intently.

Crickets chirped; tree frogs belched. But she didn't hear any telltale sign that someone was hiding there.

Had Griff made a mistake? Unlikely, despite the fact they were all human. Griff was one of the best cops she knew, tough yet fair. She'd been thrilled when he'd hired her to join his team. She inched closer to the edge of the shed and peered around the corner.

At first she didn't see anything amiss. Then she realized there was a slim figure crouched beside a woodpile. The teenager was curled up in a tight ball, as if trying to make herself invisible.

Jenna didn't think the teen was armed, but there was no point in taking any chances. Griff poked his head around the opposite corner, and she gave him a quick hand signal, indicating their quarry was there.

"Police," Jenna said, stepping around the corner and leveling her weapon at the figure hiding beside the woodpile. "Hold your hands up where I can see them."

From the corner of her eye she noticed Griff came out to join her. She kept her gaze on the small figure, relieved when two pale, slender hands slowly rose above the teen's head.

"Are you Jenna Reed?" the girl asked in a shaky voice.

Jenna blinked in surprise. How on earth did this girl know her name? "Yes. Stand up and keep your hands in the air."

The teen did as she was told.

It wasn't easy to make out the girl's facial features in the darkness, but there was no mistaking the long blond hair framing her face. "Who are you?" Jenna asked, perplexed. She didn't know her neighbors other than on a casual basis. Did this girl live somewhere nearby?

"M-my name—is—Cl-Claire."

It took Jenna a minute to realize the kid was shivering. From fear or the chill in the air—considering she wasn't wearing any sort of jacket over her ripped T-shirt—or both. The *C* engraved on the bracelet flashed in her mind. "What's your last name?"

"Towne."

"Do you have any weapons on you?" Jenna asked. "Drugs? Anything illegal?"

"N-no." The girl's thin arms began to droop with exhaustion. Griff was armed and Jenna wasn't sensing an immediate threat, so she holstered her weapon and stepped forward to pat the girl down.

Claire was excruciatingly thin, reminding Jenna of the girls who often showed up at Ruth's shelter. There was a small, nondescript cell phone in one pocket, and when Jenna moved over to the other side and patted the pocket, she heard a crinkling noise. "What's that?" she asked, dipping her fingers inside to pull out what she suspected might be a baggie containing drugs.

"N-newspaper." Claire's thin voice levered up an octave when Jenna pulled it free. "It's mine. Give it back!"

The burst of anger ironically made Jenna feel better. The girl might be down to her last few dollars, but she was still fighting, which meant she hadn't given up.

Jenna pulled out the paper, realizing it was a newspaper clipping folded over several times to make it small enough to fit in Claire's pocket. When she opened it, Jenna instantly recognized the picture of herself wearing her dress uniform as she stood in front of a crowd, thanking everyone in attendance for the donations to Ruth's shelter. She remembered that night well, because city leaders had made a big deal of her role in the recent Brookmont arrests. The article was dated just two months ago.

Well, this explained how Claire Towne knew

who she was. But there were still too many questions for her peace of mind. "Did you lose a bracelet?"

"Yes. Did you find it?" Claire's earnest face lit up at the possibility.

Jenna glanced at Griff, who was standing there with a deep frown furrowing his brow. He shrugged his shoulder as if telling her to go with her gut.

"I have it at my place." Jenna reached out to lightly grasp Claire's arm. "Come on. We need to get you out of the cold."

Claire hesitated, casting furtive glances in Griff's direction. Was the teen afraid of him?

"This is Lieutenant Vaughn, my boss," Jenna said, hoping to put Claire at ease. "Don't worry. We're not going to hurt you."

Claire's head snapped up and her fingers curled into fists. "I'm eighteen, old enough to be on my own."

"Okay," Jenna said mildly. The girl didn't look a day over sixteen. Although it could be that she looked younger in the dark because she was thin and scared.

Jenna had the distinct feeling this kid was a runaway. Although it was a mystery as to why Claire had a picture of Jenna tucked away in her back pocket.

"Do you think this is a good idea?" Griff asked in a low voice as they crossed the neighbors' lawns to head back to her place. "What if she's acting as a lure for the assailant?"

Jenna sighed, knowing he was right to be wary. But there was no way she could turn her back on this half-starved, frightened and shivering teenager. "That's why you're here to stand guard," she murmured.

Griff didn't say anything more, but he did move closer, so much so that she could feel the warmth radiating off his skin. She couldn't deny she was glad he was there. The teenager didn't say anything as they walked, but looked dejected, as if running away had sapped her strength.

As they rounded the corner of the house, Jenna slowed to a stop, realizing that she hadn't locked the front door behind her. If Griff's theory was right, the assailant could be hiding somewhere inside.

"Wait here," Jenna said, putting a hand on Griff's arm. "I need to make sure no one is inside."

"Don't leave me," Claire pleaded, grabbing the edge of Jenna's denim jacket.

"I'll go," Griff said. "She trusts you more."

That was obviously true. Jenna gave a terse nod, putting her arm around Claire's thin shoulders.

Griff headed inside, and the minute they were alone, the girl turned to Jenna. "Please, you have to help me."

Jenna was taken aback by her desperate plea. "What's wrong? Are you in trouble?"

"Yes. I need help and you're the only one I can trust. Just you, no one else. I'm so glad you're all right."

All right? Had this girl witnessed the attack? "Claire, be honest with me. Were you here earlier? Did you see that man try to grab me?"

Claire's features crumpled, and she buried her face in her hands. "Yes. I'm sorry. When that man showed up I ran away, intending to get help. But then I heard someone yell, 'Stop! Police,' so I hid in the bushes."

Jenna wasn't sure what to think of Claire's story. It certainly sounded plausible. She glanced at her modest brick house, wishing Griff would hurry. What if Claire and the masked man were working together? She pulled out her phone and mentally counted down from ten.

If Griff didn't come out soon, she was calling for backup.

Three, two, one. She lifted her phone and was about to punch in the number for their dispatcher when Griff emerged from the darkness.

"Your place is clear."

She let out a sigh and resisted the urge to close her eyes in relief. Griff was a good cop, but she couldn't deny feeling concerned about his safety. "Thanks."

He followed them inside, and she flipped on

the lights, wincing at the brightness before shutting the front door behind them. She shot the dead bolt home for added security.

She turned to face Griff and Claire. Griff was staring at Claire intently, looking a bit shaken.

"What's wrong?" She raked her gaze over Claire, who was just about Jenna's height, looking for signs of injury.

"Don't you see it?" he asked. "The resemblance is uncanny."

Resemblance? She sharpened her gaze on Claire's face and took a step back as the realization hit hard.

Seeing Claire's face was akin to looking at her own reflection in the mirror.

Griff didn't like this situation one bit. First the assault, then this girl showing up, looking far too much like Jenna.

On closer inspection Claire was definitely younger than Jenna by several years, so they couldn't be twins. And there were very subtle differences in their appearances. Claire's hair was lighter in color and longer than Jenna's. But the similarities of their facial features, down to the shape of their clear blue eyes, made him wonder if they were related in some way.

But Jenna claimed to be an only child. And he didn't think that was a lie. Considering the way she was gaping at Claire, she was just as stunned to see the girl as he was.

"Okay, Claire, you better start talking," Jenna said with a dark scowl. "You told me you were in trouble. What kind of trouble? Did you steal something? Get caught? Run away? What?"

She was firing questions faster than her M16 shot bullets, and Griff watched Claire's shoulders droop as if she were exhausted.

"Maybe we should offer her something to eat?" The emaciated look of Claire bothered him. "She looks hungry."

Jenna let out a huff but then nodded. "Right. Food. I'll throw in a frozen pizza."

The way she hurried into the other room made him think she was anxious to get away from Claire. Honestly, he understood. He'd heard that they all had a double in the world, but he hadn't really believed it.

Until now. The physical similarities between the girls were eerie.

Claire was subtly inching away from him, rubbing her hands over her arms. He grabbed an afghan off the sofa and tossed it to her. "Wrap up. You'll feel warm soon."

She nodded and did as she was told, huddling into the blanket as if she could disappear inside. He raked a hand over his short hair.

Now what?

"Do you live in the Milwaukee area?" he asked.

Claire shrugged but didn't answer. She was looking at him as if he was an ogre, so he tried to soften his harsh features.

"Listen, we're not going to hurt you, okay? We just need to understand what's going on. Jenna was brutally attacked a few hours ago and we need to know why. Are you in town with someone?"

Claire slowly shook her head from side to side. When she finally spoke, her voice was so soft he had to strain to hear her. "I came on my own. Took a bus from Chicago."

Chicago? He found it hard to believe this tiny slip of a girl came ninety miles with nothing more than the clothes on her back and a crumpled piece of newspaper in her pocket.

Being a runaway was looking more and more likely. Especially since she seemed to be afraid of him.

Because he was a cop? A man? Both?

She hadn't seemed afraid of Jenna. In fact, he was amazed the girl had gone out of her way to purposefully find Jenna.

But how?

"Do you have any identification? Anything to prove who you are?"

Claire shook her head again, easing toward the opening leading to the kitchen.

"Okay, why don't you tell me how you found Jenna?"

She shook her head and darted a glance toward

the door. He bit back a sigh of frustration. How could he get this girl to trust him?

"Pizza's in, should be ready in a few minutes." Jenna looked at Claire. "Come into the kitchen. I think you owe us an explanation, don't you?"

The enticing aroma of pepperoni, cheese and tomato sauce filled the air, and Claire was practically drooling with anticipation. But then she hesitated. "I need to use the bathroom to wash up."

"Sure. It's down the hall to your right."

"Thank you." Claire slipped away, leaving Griff and Jenna alone in the kitchen.

A strained moment stretched between them.

"Do you think it's possible you're related to her in some way?" he asked, breaking the silence.

"I don't see how, although I guess she could be a cousin. I don't know much about my father's side of the family."

Griff lifted a brow. "I don't think cousins share that kind of resemblance."

Jenna scowled at him. "Listen, this isn't your problem. It's mine. There's no reason for you to stick around. I can handle this from here."

"Funny, I was thinking we should take her down to the station, maybe check her fingerprints for missing persons."

"Why? The only crime we're aware of is trespassing."

"*That we're aware of* is the key phrase, don't you think?"

Jenna's chin thrust forward stubbornly. "Plenty of time for all that later. Right now she needs food, warmth and shelter."

Griff didn't like the idea of leaving Jenna here alone. The girl was young and looked harmless, but that didn't mean much. He knew only too well that looks could be deceiving. His parents were proof of that. Innocent people had trusted them with their life's savings when they shouldn't have.

Then he focused on her last word. "Shelter. That's a great idea. Why don't you take her to Ruth's?"

"Lately her place has been running full," Jenna pointed out. "Although I guess I could call to see if there are any openings."

"No!" Claire said from the doorway, looking so pale Griff feared she might crumple to the floor at any moment.

"It's okay, Claire," Jenna said in a soothing voice. "We were just trying to think of ways to keep you safe."

"I'm safer here with you," the girl protested. "I don't want to go to a shelter."

Griff tried to stifle a weary sigh. From the compassionate expression in Jenna's eyes, he suspected she wanted to give in to Claire's wishes.

"I won't force you, Claire. We'll be fine," Jenna assured him. "She can hang out here for what's left of the night."

"Oh, yeah?" Griff wanted to shake some sense into Jenna. "What if that guy shows up again to finish what he's started?"

"Stop it—you're frightening Claire," Jenna admonished him. "Besides, I doubt he is going to come back. And if he does, I'm armed and will call for backup."

He stared at her, trying to find a way to convince Jenna that keeping a strange teenager in her home wasn't smart. "You don't know Claire isn't involved in this," he finally reminded her. "If you're letting her stay, then I'm staying, too."

Jenna looked taken aback by his declaration, but to his surprise, Claire nodded. "That's good."

Good? He frowned. "Why? Do you know something about the guy who attacked Jenna?"

Claire shifted uncomfortably, looking guilty. "I'm afraid so."

He knew it! "Start talking," he advised in a gruff voice.

Claire swallowed hard, her gaze darting between him and Jenna. It was several long seconds before she spoke. "I think that guy attacked Jenna by mistake."

"By mistake?" Griff echoed in surprise. He'd never expected her to say something that crazy. "What makes you think that?"

Claire licked her dry lips. "I managed to escape from them, so I'm pretty sure they're looking for me."

Griff looked at Jenna, struck again by the similarities between the two women. Maybe Claire's statement wasn't that far-fetched.

Jenna's eyes widened in shock. "I guess it's possible the masked man made a mistake."

"That doesn't explain why the bulb was removed from your porch light," Griff pointed out. "If he's the one who removed it, then he had to know you lived here."

Claire winced. "That was me," she said in a soft voice. "I removed the lightbulb, needing darkness while I waited for Jenna to come home." The teen's eyes filled with tears as she moved toward Jenna, who placed a consoling arm around her thin shoulders. "I'm sorry. I never meant for you to be hurt."

Griff stared helplessly at the two of them. If Claire was telling the truth and the assailant really had mistaken Jenna for Claire, then she and Jenna were still in danger.

Leaving him to figure out how to protect them both.

# FOUR

"So you must have lost your bracelet while you were removing the lightbulb," Jenna murmured, trying to come to grips with what Claire had revealed. To be honest, she was relieved the guy had attacked her instead of Claire. There was no way the younger girl would have had the strength to fight him off.

The fact that Claire had escaped from the guy before also explained why the attack had been so personal. Why he'd seemed so intent on using physical force against her.

"You mentioned escaping from danger. What exactly happened?" Jenna asked.

Claire lifted her thin, bony shoulders in a shrug. "It's a long story, but basically I escaped being drugged and forced into prostitution."

Jenna gasped and curled her fingers into fists. It was too easy to imagine how scared Claire had been.

"Who did that to you? Do you have names?

Where did this happen?" Griff asked, going into full lieutenant mode.

Claire shrank against Jenna, convincing her that the teen wouldn't want to relay horrible details in front of a guy.

"I don't want to talk about it," Claire whispered.

"It's okay. We'll have time to go into that later," she assured the girl. Then she turned to Griff, imploring him to back off. "The most important thing right now is to get Claire someplace safe. Now that we know she's still in danger, we need a different plan. I guess you were right. Going to the women's shelter tonight is likely our best option."

Claire let out a soft sound of distress, but Jenna did her best to ignore it.

"Agreed," Griff said firmly. "You can give me directions and I'll take you both there. Because you're still in danger, as well, Jenna."

He was crazy if he thought she was going to hide out in some women's shelter. "I can't let you do that," Jenna protested. "The location of the shelter is secret and needs to stay that way. The women who live there don't trust men, even cops. But they know me. I've been supporting them for years. I'll take Claire there on my own."

Griff stared at her, concern wrinkling his brow. "I don't think that's smart," he protested. "What if that guy comes back here looking for you?"

"I'll make sure we're not followed, and then I'll find someplace else to stay for what's left of the night."

"I don't like it," Griff said in a burst of exasperation. "You know as well as I do that I'm not going to breach the security of the shelter. There's no reason for you to be so paranoid."

"Paranoid? The women in the shelter fear for their lives and the lives of their children," she pointed out, striving for patience. "I don't understand what your problem is. You really think an armed sheriff's deputy isn't capable of taking a young woman to a shelter?"

Griff let out a heavy sigh and scrubbed his hands over his face, giving Jenna the satisfaction of knowing she'd made her point.

Her boss might not like it, but he clearly wouldn't stand in her way. Yeah, she appreciated his help, but it was time he proved he actually trusted her abilities.

Instead of treating her like a victim.

Griff hated to admit Jenna was right. If she were any other deputy, he wouldn't be standing here arguing about this. "Fine. I'll head out, but I want you to keep in touch."

"Will do. Thanks for your help."

Griff turned and walked through the small house to the front door.

He flipped the dead bolt open, then glanced over his shoulder. "Lock up behind me."

Griff waited until Jenna came over before stepping outside. When he heard the door lock snap into place behind him, he made his way across the grass toward the spot where he'd left his vehicle.

He pulled his keys out of his pocket but fumbled and dropped them. When he bent down to pick them up, he heard the same diesel-engine clicking noise from earlier.

He froze for several long seconds, his thoughts racing. The man who was after Claire? Maybe.

Staying low, Griff headed over toward his police-issued vehicle, using the frame for cover. When he peeked out, he could see there was a dark van, either blue, black or gray, rolling down the street without any headlights blazing.

Something wasn't right with this picture, and he was relieved Jenna and Claire were safe inside. From what he could tell, there was only the driver, so he popped out from behind his car with his gun raised.

"Stop! Police! Get out of the vehicle."

The car stopped. He waited as the driver's window slowly rolled down. Before Griff could move, he saw the short barrel of a handgun. He dived to the ground mere seconds before bullets whizzed through the air, echoing through the night.

The assailant was shooting at him. At a cop!

He rolled closer to the edge of his vehicle and then eased up to a crouch. Every one of his senses was on red alert as he leveled his weapon at the sound of the diesel engine. But the driver had shot into Reverse, speeding backward away from him.

In a flash, the van executed a crazy, tire-squealing turn and disappeared out of sight.

Griff stood for a minute, his heart pounding with adrenaline. Had the man fired at him to scare him off?

Or had he recognized Griff as the cop who'd rescued Jenna earlier?

If that was the case, he had to believe the guy in the car fully intended to kill him.

Jenna heard the distinctive sound of gunfire and quickly grabbed her weapon, pulling Claire behind her. She reached for her phone, intending to call for backup.

She paused when she heard a loud pounding at her front door. "It's Griff. Open up!"

"Stay here," she whispered to Claire before she darted over to unlock and open the door. Griff barreled inside, his face pulled into a fierce mask of anger.

"What happened? Are you okay?" she asked in a rush, trying to look for any sign of injury.

"Where's Claire?" He brushed past her to head into the kitchen, where Claire was standing up against the wall, a half-eaten slice of pizza left sitting on the table.

Jenna winced at the way Claire shrank away from him, clearly afraid.

"Where's your phone?" he demanded.

"In my pocket, but it's shut off, see?" The teen pulled it out and showed him the black screen. "I keep it off so no one can track it."

"The phone can be tracked, even if it's shut off," Jenna said, peering over his shoulder.

He took the phone, turned it on and scrolled through the recent numbers. "There don't seem to be any calls made in the last twenty-four hours," he muttered.

Jenna lifted a brow, not sure why he thought there would be. Claire was hiding secrets, but the stark fear in the girl's eyes was all too real.

"Jenna's right. The guy who's after you can track you by pinging this phone," Griff said grimly. "We have to get rid of it, for your safety and ours."

Claire winced but didn't protest when he pulled the battery out and tossed the phone in the trash.

"Come on. We need to get out of here."

"Tell me what happened," Jenna demanded. "Who was shooting?"

"I suspect it was the same guy who attacked you."

"Why?" Jenna asked.

"I saw a car rolling slowly down the street with its lights off. I heard a similar car engine earlier when we were sweeping your yard right after the attack. When I confronted him, he opened fire."

"He actually tried to kill you?" Jenna felt sick, knowing that she'd inadvertently put Griff in danger.

Claire gasped and went even more pale than normal. "We have to get away! Please don't take me to the shelter, either."

Jenna wavered, second-guessing her earlier decision. It might be better to keep Claire with her. And right now they needed to get far away from her place. "Okay, pack up the food. I'll grab some clothes and toiletries."

"I'll take care of the food. Just hurry," Griff urged.

Jenna ran upstairs with Claire close on her heels. "I can help," she said, although Jenna suspected the real reason Claire followed her was because she was still afraid of Griff.

"Here, wear this," Jenna said, tossing a dark sweatshirt at her. "Then head into the bathroom to grab toiletries." Jenna picked up a duffel bag and started stashing clothing inside. Claire was thin, but Jenna made sure to toss in enough clothes for her, too, including a belt so the jeans wouldn't fall off her slim hips. Within minutes Jenna had everything they needed, and they returned to the kitchen to find Griff waiting impatiently.

He was holding a tinfoil-covered plate, and when she approached, he took the duffel from her fingers and slung it over his shoulder. "I'm going to drive around to the alley. I need you and Claire to wait near the back door until you see me. Keep your weapon handy."

Jenna nodded. "Okay, but be careful."

Griff gave a curt nod. "I honestly believe they're gone. For the moment."

Jenna silently agreed and shut off all the inside lights as she followed Griff to the front door. Once he slipped through the opening, she shut the door and slid the dead bolt home.

She returned to the kitchen, where Claire waited, looking dwarfish in the oversize sweatshirt.

"Come on. Stay close," Jenna said. She tucked Claire behind her as she opened the back door. Gun in hand, she peered into the darkness, waiting for Griff to arrive.

Jenna took her time scanning the backyard for any sign of the assailant. She agreed with Griff that the guy probably wouldn't return anytime soon, but that didn't mean she was going to take any unnecessary risks. Especially if the guy was really after Claire.

The sound of a car engine grew louder, and she tensed, making sure the vehicle was Griff's. She spotted the light rack running along the roof and let her breath out in a soundless sigh of relief.

He paused in the alley, waiting for them. Jenna knew it was time to move. "Keep close behind me," she instructed Claire. "We're going to stay in the shadows as much as possible."

"Okay," Claire whispered, curling her fingers into the back of Jenna's denim jacket.

Jenna led the way outside and skirted the patio to make her way through the backyard. Claire hovered so close, she accidentally stepped on the back of Jenna's shoe, causing them both to stumble a bit.

They reached the alley without incident. Jenna yanked open the back passenger door for Claire, making sure the girl was safely inside before sliding into the front seat beside Griff. The moment she closed the door behind her, Griff hit the gas.

"Where are we going?" Jenna asked when Griff made several turns, first heading in one direction and then switching course to head in another. "I suppose you're taking us to the police station?"

"I should, but I'm not willing to do that yet. Not until I understand what's going on."

Jenna could barely hide her surprise. Griff always followed the rules. "A hotel, then?"

Griff shook his head. "We're heading to my place."

His place? She tried to hide her shock. "Don't you think a hotel would be safer?"

"No. I believe the guy shot at me because I'm the one who interrupted the assault on you, but there's no way he could know my name or where I live. I have a spare bedroom that you and Claire can share." He paused, then added, "Besides, it's almost dawn and we need sleep. In the morning we'll use my computer to start investigating the mess that we've stumbled into."

Jenna couldn't argue his logic, even though the thought of going to Griff's place was unnerving. She was capable of taking care of herself and Claire, but considering the fact that Griff was now in danger, as well, he was right to encourage them to stick together.

She glanced back at Claire. "Are you okay with the plan?"

Claire nodded. "As long as you're there with me," she said in a quiet voice.

"I will be," Jenna promised. She turned back around. "All right, then. I guess that's settled."

Griff drove for several more miles, then doubled back, before pulling into his driveway. He parked in the garage, and Jenna waited until the garage door closed before unbuckling her seat belt and pushing open the door.

She looked into the back, surprised to see Claire's head propped against the window, her eyes closed as if she'd finally given in to the exhaustion that plagued her. There were pizza crumbs scattered across her lap, indicating she had helped herself to some leftovers. Jenna was relieved the girl had food in her system.

For a moment Jenna simply stared at her, wondering about this young woman who looked so much like her.

"Need help?" Griff asked.

"No, thanks." Jenna pulled herself up short and opened the car door, shaking Claire awake. "Come on. We need to go inside."

Claire blinked in confusion, but nodded. She struggled to get out of the car, managing with Jenna's help to stand on her own two feet.

Griff led the way, flipping lights on as he went. Jenna was curious about the place her boss called home, but tried not to be too nosy.

"The first door on the right upstairs is the guest bedroom, and the bathroom is across the hall," he said. Then he frowned when he realized Claire was sagging heavily against Jenna. "I was hoping we'd get some more information out of her tonight."

Jenna shook her head. "You're the one who

pointed out it's almost dawn. She's not going anywhere. It's better for her to get some rest."

Griff nodded reluctantly, took the duffel bag upstairs and set it inside the guest bedroom. Then he hesitated near the doorway. "Good night, Jenna."

"Good night, Griff."

He surprised her by flashing a devastatingly handsome smile before turning to leave them alone in the room. Jenna stared after him for a moment, trying to understand why he'd looked so happy.

It took a few seconds to realize she'd broken her self-imposed rule by calling him by his first name.

And for the life of her, she couldn't understand why her slip would make him smile.

Griff managed to get a couple of hours of sleep before his internal alarm clock kicked in. He dragged himself out of bed and felt a little more human after a quick shower. He pulled on a pair of black jeans and a black SWAT sweatshirt.

There was no sound coming from the guest bedroom, so he headed down to the kitchen to brew a pot of coffee. He still had trouble wrapping his mind around the fact that the assailant had tried to kill him. Claire's escape must be a significant threat if the guy wanted her back badly enough to risk shooting a cop.

After gathering eggs from the fridge, he began breaking them into a large bowl. Working in the kitchen wasn't his strong suit, but he could manage to throw something edible together so they wouldn't starve. Ham-and-cheese omelets with toast would have to suffice.

While the omelet was cooking, he took a sip of his coffee, nearly spilling it down the front of his sweatshirt when he noticed Jenna standing in the doorway.

"Good morning. That coffee smells good."

He pulled himself together and gestured toward the pot. "Help yourself. Breakfast will be ready soon."

"Looks great," she said, opening the cupboards to search for a mug. She poured a cup of coffee and then rummaged in the fridge for milk.

Watching Jenna making herself at home in his kitchen created an intimacy he wished he hadn't noticed. In the last year of his marriage, there hadn't been many Saturday mornings like this. Helen worked way too many hours at the law firm, including weekends, even the ones he happened to be off duty.

Griff concentrated on making sure the omelet didn't burn, then turned to push the toaster handle down. Jenna was standing so close he could smell the strawberry scent that seemed to cling to her skin.

He gave himself a mental shake, reminding

himself that she and Claire were in danger. He couldn't afford to be sidetracked.

Especially not by a woman who reported to him. A woman who reminded him of a life he didn't deserve to have.

A few minutes later the food was ready and he was relieved when Jenna took the seat across from him. When she bowed her head to pray, he remembered his grandmother doing the same thing and found himself looking down at his hands as he waited for her to finish.

"We need some sort of game plan." Jenna dug into her omelet and took a bite. "Wow, this is good."

"You were expecting poison?" he asked drily.

She laughed, the husky sound sending shivers of awareness down his spine. "No, of course not. I just didn't realize you were a great cook."

He wasn't, but quickly filled his own mouth with food so he wouldn't make a bigger fool out of himself.

"Claire's hiding something," Jenna continued as if she hadn't knocked him sideways with her laugh. "I understand she's scared, but we need to know exactly what we're up against."

"I'm sure she'll cooperate now that she's safe," he said.

Jenna took another bite, looking thoughtful. "I don't know. I get the feeling there's more to her situation than she wants to tell us."

Griff frowned. "Are you saying you think she may have participated in something illegal?"

Jenna sighed and pinched the bridge of her nose in a familiar gesture. "Yeah. I hate to say it, but that's the vibe I'm getting."

He always told his deputies to trust their instincts. Jenna in particular knew how to read abused women. If she thought there was something else going on, then he believed her. "Maybe you should talk to her alone."

She glanced up at him in surprise. "Really?"

He knew better than to micromanage his team. "Yeah. Why not? Claire trusts you."

"Okay." She took a sip of coffee. "Have to admit, it was creepy finding that newspaper clipping of me in her pocket."

He couldn't agree more. "I'll start a background check on her while you two talk. Hopefully there isn't a warrant out for her arrest."

Jenna's expression turned grim. "I guess I wouldn't be too surprised if there was."

There was a muffled thump from upstairs, indicating Claire was awake. Griff finished his breakfast and then rose to his feet, intending to make Claire's omelet.

"Good morning, Claire." Jenna greeted the girl as she hesitantly stepped into the kitchen. "Help yourself to coffee."

The girl wrinkled her nose and slipped into

the vacant chair closest to Jenna. "No, thanks. I'd rather have a diet cola."

Griff took a soft drink from the fridge and handed it to Claire, noticing she was wearing her charm bracelet. It didn't take long for Jenna to comment on it, too.

"Who gave you the bracelet?" she asked. "A boyfriend?"

Claire paled and shook her head. "No, my mother gave it to me shortly before the stupid woman from child protective services took me away from her. It's all I have left."

Now it was Jenna's turn to go pale. She pushed her plate away and wrapped her fingers around her coffee mug as if craving warmth. "What happened to your mother?"

Claire grimaced. "I don't know. I'm going to try and find her." Jenna lifted a curious brow. "I know she had problems, but they had no right to take me away."

"Drugs? Alcohol?"

"Drugs," Claire admitted with a heavy sigh. "She'd stay clean for a while, but then one day I'd come home from school and find her strung out."

Griff tightened his grip on the spatula, imagining what Claire had suffered. Maybe she had broken the law at some point. He only hoped that the crime wasn't so bad he couldn't help her get out of it.

He slid the omelet onto a plate, added toast

and set it beside Claire. She glanced up and gave him a nod of thanks.

Jenna paused for a few minutes, allowing her to eat. Claire eagerly dug into the simple meal, making Griff glad that he'd taken the time to cook a hot breakfast.

He'd fully intended to leave them alone, but since Claire seemed willing to keep talking, he decided to clean up the kitchen a bit, admittedly eavesdropping on their conversation.

"How old were you when you entered the foster system?" Jenna asked in a gentle tone.

"Eleven, almost twelve, and I hated every minute of it," Claire said flatly. "My mother's rights were terminated a year later. I was adopted by an older couple, but I didn't handle it well. I caused a lot of trouble for them, so I couldn't really blame them for giving me up for re-adoption."

Jenna shot him a puzzled look, and he shook his head, indicating he wasn't sure what Claire was talking about.

"But that isn't really important right now," Claire said before taking another bite of her omelet. "I wanted to talk to you about my mother, Georgina Towne."

Jenna leaned forward and nodded. "Okay, what about her?"

Claire looked disappointed. "Her name doesn't sound familiar to you?"

"No, why?"

Claire's shoulders slumped. "Because she's your mother, too. She had another child several years before me. A daughter named Jennifer, who was also taken away from her. I saw photographs."

Jenna sucked in a harsh breath. "What are you talking about?"

"You're my sister, Jenna. The minute I saw your picture in the newspaper, I knew you were my long-lost sister. That's why I came to find you."

Griff couldn't say he was totally surprised. He'd thought from the moment he laid eyes on Claire that she was related to Jenna.

But the shocked denial on Jenna's face indicated she didn't agree. In fact, she jumped up, shoving her chair back so abruptly it toppled over onto the floor, and ran out of the room as if she could outrun the words Claire had spoken.

# FIVE

Jenna ran upstairs and darted into the bathroom, closing and locking the door firmly behind her. She collapsed onto the commode and stared down at her trembling fingers.

No way was Claire her sister. Jenna knew her mother was Anna Marie Reed, not Georgina whatever. And her name was Jenna, not Jennifer.

She wasn't adopted.

Surely her mother would have told her if she was?

For a moment she buried her face in her hands, trying to block out Claire's blunt statement. The girl was likely just making up a family connection because they looked so much alike. Yeah, that was it. Claire must have seen her picture in the paper and become determined to find her. Claire was only imagining that Jenna was her long-lost older sister.

Jenna thought back to her earliest childhood memories. Her mother telling her to be quiet because her father was sleeping. Her mother pushing Jenna behind her when her father started yelling.

Not too surprising that her clearest memories were linked to being afraid of her father.

She didn't remember being with any other woman but her mother. Certainly not some woman who did drugs. But then she remembered the day she pulled a photo album out from under her parents' bed, anxious to see pictures of herself and her parents when she was a baby. Surely they must have been happy at one point in their marriage?

Only there weren't any photographs of her as an infant.

When she'd asked her mother why they didn't have any pictures of them as a family from when she was a baby, her mother explained that there had been a fire in their apartment building when Jenna was five years old and the photographs were damaged beyond repair.

Jenna had believed her at the time.

But what if the truth was that there weren't any photographs because she'd been adopted when she was five years old?

Was her bracelet a legacy from her birth mother?

A firm rap on the door made her lift her head. "Jenna?" Griff's husky voice permeated the door. "Are you all right?"

No, she wasn't all right. But, of course, she did her best to shove her frayed emotions aside. "Yes. I'll be out in a minute."

She drew in a deep breath and let it out slowly. Right now, it didn't matter much whether Claire was really her sister. A masked man had assaulted her and shot at Griff. They needed to stay focused on investigating who was after them and why Claire came to find her in the first place.

Jenna splashed water on her face, then opened the door. Griff stood there, his dark gaze searching hers. She was shocked by how badly she wanted to throw herself into his arms.

"I'm fine," she repeated, forcing a smile. "Give me some time alone with Claire to find out more about the man she escaped from."

She moved to brush past him, but Griff stopped her with a hand on her arm, the warmth of his palm radiating through the fabric of her sweater. "Jenna, I know meeting Claire like this has been a shock, but we could request a DNA sample if you really want to know for certain."

She hesitated, then shrugged. "I'll think about it. I hate to say it, but she may be right. My parents didn't have any photographs of me as a baby. Nothing, in fact, until I was in kindergarten. But finding out the truth about my past isn't our top priority."

Griff looked down at her for a long moment,

giving Jenna the impression she could lose herself in his dark gaze. "I'm here if you need me."

The simple offer of support took her breath away. She couldn't remember the last time she'd leaned on anyone. Certainly not Eric. Or her father.

Although she shouldn't be leaning on Griff, either. She was strong enough to stand on her own. "Thanks," she managed, before taking a step away. His hand dropped from her arm, and she immediately missed the warmth of his touch.

She headed back downstairs, telling herself to stop being ridiculous. Being in close proximity to Griff was playing tricks on her psyche.

Claire was still seated at the kitchen table, hunched over her half-finished plate. Jenna refilled her coffee mug, sensing she was going to need the extra boost of caffeine. She returned to the table, sitting beside Claire.

"Finish your breakfast," she suggested. "We have a lot to talk about."

Claire sniffed as if fighting tears and picked up her fork. "I thought you'd be happy to have a sister."

Jenna's heart squeezed in her chest. "I am happy to have a sister. It's just that I didn't even know I was adopted. You need to give me a little time to adjust, Claire."

Claire brightened at the news and resumed

eating. Jenna waited until she'd finished her omelet before pressing Claire for more information.

"I need you to start at the very beginning," she said when Claire set down her fork. "And I'd like to take notes, if that's okay with you."

Claire gave a jerky nod, so Jenna stood and rummaged through Griff's kitchen drawers, looking for paper and a pen. She found what she needed and returned to the table.

"Okay, you said that you were adopted by an older couple. What were their names?" Jenna asked.

"Judy and Bob Bronson. I lived with them for about five years, until I was sixteen. I lied earlier—I'm still only sixteen. I'll turn seventeen in a few weeks. But Judy and Bob decided I was too much trouble for them, so they put me up for re-adoption."

Jenna frowned. "You mentioned that before, but I've never heard of it."

"Me, either, but they put some sort of advertisement up online and then heard from a lawyer. A younger couple came by, telling me how much they'd like to be my new parents. I didn't want to go with them, but Judy and Bob didn't give me much of a choice." Bitterness shimmered through Claire's tone.

"It doesn't make sense," Jenna agreed. "If you're almost seventeen, why not hang in there another year until you turn eighteen, then kick you out?"

"I don't know, but the minute we drove away, I knew I was in trouble. The guy dropped off the woman and then tied my wrists together. When I asked what was going on, he told me he was taking me someplace *special*."

Jenna's stomach tightened, dreading what she knew would come next. "Where?"

Claire shoved her empty plate out of the way in a rare display of anger. "Some stupid apartment building a few miles off the interstate. There were a couple of other girls there. The expressions in their eyes reminded me of the way my mom looked when she was on drugs. I was so afraid, but then one of the girls slipped me a small penknife and told me to save myself before the guy took her and the others away."

Jenna could imagine all too well how the plan would be to get the girls hooked on drugs to the point they'd do whatever was necessary to get their next fix. Even if that meant giving a penknife away to someone else, rather than using it to escape.

"When he came back, I lunged at him, stabbing his neck with the knife. He lost his footing and fell backward, hitting his head on the edge of the coffee table. There was so much blood…" Claire's voice trailed off and she raised dull blue eyes to meet Jenna's. "I'm pretty sure I killed him."

Jenna reached out and put her arm around Claire's slim shoulders. "Don't worry, Claire," she murmured, giving the girl, who might very well be her sister, a hug. She silently thanked God for watching over Claire. What the girl described was the stuff nightmares were made of. "We'll figure this out."

Claire leaned against Jenna and nodded. "I took his phone out of his pocket along with some cash and ran. I ran and ran until I was far enough away to hitch a ride to Chicago. But in the city I caught a bus to Milwaukee so I could find you."

"I'm glad you did," Jenna said firmly. "There's no reason you should have to deal with these guys alone." Her mind reeled from what Claire described. Human trafficking? She'd seen headlines stating that it was a problem closer to home than anyone realized, but to know Claire had almost been forced into prostitution—or worse—made her shiver.

"Don't tell your boss," Claire whispered, swiping at her eyes and pushing away from Jenna. "He'll arrest me for killing that guy. I'd feel better if we could go off on our own."

"Griff won't arrest you, Claire," Jenna assured her. "Trust me, he's a really nice guy. He cares about fighting crime as much as I do. And I know he'll do everything in his power to find the men who did this." She reached up and smoothed the damp hair away from Claire's cheek. "Besides, you don't know for sure that guy is dead. Could be you just knocked him unconscious."

Claire's blue eyes widened with hope. "You really think so?"

Jenna had no way of knowing for sure, but she nodded. "It's not easy to kill someone with a penknife, but even if he is dead, you fought against him in self-defense because you feared for your life, which is all that matters."

Claire's expression filled with relief. "I was so afraid you'd send me back. They have papers saying I belong to them."

Jenna clenched her jaw in a flash of anger. The couple who put Claire up for re-adoption was just as much to blame as the guy who ultimately took custody of her. Kids didn't belong to anyone. They were precious gifts from God. But she knew, all too well, that some people didn't value their kids.

Her father certainly hadn't.

"I doubt whatever papers they have are legal, but right now, we need to focus on the facts. Do you know anything about the guy you fought to get away from?"

"He claimed his name was Stuart Trent and the woman was Debra, his wife. But I doubt those are their real names," Claire wisely pointed out.

"Maybe not," Jenna agreed, scribbling more notes on the pad of paper. "But it's a place to start."

Claire pinched her nose for a moment, then sighed. "I know I shouldn't have lied to you about my age. But I promise not to be a problem anymore," she said. "Please don't give me away."

Jenna tossed the pen aside and drew Claire into a hug. "I won't," she promised, catching a glimpse of Griff standing in the doorway with such a grim expression on his face she knew that he must have overheard at least part of the conversation. "You're stuck with me," she added.

Jenna didn't need a DNA test to prove they were sisters. A blood relationship didn't matter. There was no way she could turn her back on Claire.

They were in this together.

Griff didn't want to intrude on the intense conversation between Claire and Jenna, but he stewed about how Jenna was handling the possibility Claire was really her sister, to the point he couldn't stay away.

He'd finished the background check on Claire and discovered she had quite the juvie record. Shoplifting, breaking and entering, and disorderly conduct, to name a few. Nothing so bad that she couldn't recover, if she kept her promise about staying out of trouble.

Griff had spent some time investigating the concept of *re-adopting*, as well. Claire's story wasn't the only one, and what had bothered him the most had been the babies and toddlers. Couples adopted children from Russia, China or Korea, only to discover the kids were more than they'd bargained for. So they took the easy way out, giving the kids up for re-adoption. Unfortunately, the people taking these kids no one else wanted weren't the upstanding citizens you'd hope for. All too often, these kids ended up in the hands of abusers, or worse, pedophiles. The very idea of it made him sick.

Claire was safe with Jenna, but what about the other girls she'd seen? He needed to find the local ringleaders of the human-trafficking ring and bring them down, arresting every last one of them.

Still, they didn't have much to go on. He hovered in the doorway, wondering if Jenna had been able to get any more concrete evidence.

Claire and Jenna broke apart, Claire wiping her eyes on the sleeve of her oversize sweatshirt. "Tell you what," Jenna said in a cheerful voice. "Let's take a break for a bit. Since Griff cooked breakfast, it's our turn to think of something for lunch."

The teen nodded and rose to her feet. Jenna went to Griff and handed him her notes. "It's not much," she murmured. "But it's worth a shot."

Jenna looked exhausted, as if the emotional scene had taken a lot out of her. Did the same thing happen when she helped the women at the shelter? He suspected it did. He squashed the urge to pull her into his arms, comforting her the same way she had supported Claire.

"If this is the name he used to re-adopt Claire, then there's bound to be some sort of paper trail. I'll get started on this right away."

"Sounds good." Jenna's wan smile tugged at his heart. "You could also try reassuring her you're not about to arrest her. That's the main reason she's afraid of you."

The news made him feel marginally better. At least it wasn't him personally, just the fact that he was a cop. "I will," he promised.

The day passed slowly; performing in-depth searches was tedious work. Griff was glad it was Saturday so he wasn't expected at the office, but he also knew it wasn't likely that they'd get this wrapped up in a few days.

Should he call his boss, the deputy chief of operations? Herb Markham was planning to retire at the end of the year and made it clear that Griff was a viable candidate for his job.

At least, he had been in the running. Now that he hadn't followed the rules, starting from when Jenna had been attacked, he doubted that was still the case.

He wanted to believe that Herb would still

provide him a decent reference, even if he took a few days off to work the case on his own time. Handing the investigation over to someone else wasn't an option. But he knew that was exactly what Herb would expect, especially since he'd become personally involved.

No, he wasn't going to give up the case. Even if that meant ruining his career. He'd just have to hope for the best. Especially since no one else had his passion for upholding the law. Even after all these years, he still felt the need to atone for his parents' mistakes, for the pyramid scheme they'd created to bilk innocent people out of their hard-earned money.

Claire and Jenna had made thick sandwiches for lunch, depleting the contents of his fridge. He pulled out brats and burgers for dinner, then made a mental note to hit the grocery store first thing in the morning.

But Jenna clearly had other ideas. "I'd like to attend church services tomorrow," she said, as he set a plate of food on the table.

"Um, okay. Where do you go?" he asked.

"The same place as everyone else," she said, as if that explained everything. "You know, the church down the street from the American Lodge Motel."

He nodded in understanding, then glanced at Claire. "Are you going, too?"

Claire didn't look overly thrilled, but she nodded. "I figure it can't hurt, right?"

The teen had a point. He swallowed a sigh, wishing he could avoid taking them, but no way was he going to let them go out alone. It wasn't Jenna's fault that he hadn't set foot in a church since Helen died.

Griff stared down at his plate for a long moment, wrestling with his conscience. He didn't need to go inside the church. He could drop them off and wait for them in the car.

Yeah, and what excuse would he use? He told himself to stop being an idiot. Claire was right. What could it hurt to go inside and sit through a service?

"Sure," he answered when he realized Jenna was watching him closely. "What time?"

"Ten thirty, and thanks. This means a lot to me."

Jenna's blue gaze shimmered with empathy. Her eyes saw way too much.

"I've struck out so far on finding anything about Stuart Trent," he said. "But I intend to keep looking."

"I wonder if we should ask the Chicago PD for help," Jenna said between bites of her hamburger. "They might have a line on this trafficking ring already."

"More likely the FBI," Griff corrected her. "But I can call the Chicago office, too."

Jenna wrinkled her nose. "If you do that, the Feds will take the case away from us."

"Maybe," he agreed, understanding her trepidation. "But we don't want to stumble into the middle of their investigation, either."

Jenna was silent for a moment. "After church, I think we should stop in and talk to Judy and Bob Bronson."

Claire sucked in a loud breath. "No, I don't want to see them!"

Jenna grimaced. "I know, but that's where this mess started, right?"

Claire nodded reluctantly. "Yeah, I guess."

"I think we need to find out what paperwork they have from Stuart Trent."

"That's a good idea," Griff said, glancing at his watch. Was it too late to head over there tonight? "I'll find out where they're located."

"I can give you their address and take you there, too." Claire had begun to warm up to him over the course of the day. "They're on the south side of Milwaukee."

"Maybe we should go now, right after dinner," Jenna said, obviously anxious to jump-start their investigation.

But Claire was shaking her head. "They won't be home. They play bingo on Saturday nights."

Bingo? Just how old was this couple? Griff decided it was better not to ask. "That's fine. Tomorrow is soon enough."

After they finished eating dinner and taking care of the dishes, Claire excused herself and disappeared into the guest bedroom. Jenna took a seat beside him, looking over his shoulder as he searched on the computer. He wanted to tell her not to sit so close because her strawberry scent was already permanently fixed in his brain, but knew he was being overly sensitive.

After an hour, Jenna sighed and ground the heels of her hands over her eyes. "I'm so tired I can't see straight," she confessed.

He nodded. "Yeah, I keep reading the same words over and over again. I guess we should call it a night."

"Sounds good." She looked as if she wanted to say something more, but rose to her feet and padded silently from the room.

He listened to her footsteps climbing the stairs, then shut down his computer. No one had slept more than four hours earlier that morning, so it only made sense to call it an early night.

At least they were safe here.

Griff poured a large glass of water, then flipped off the lights. Just as he was about to leave the kitchen, he heard a muffled thud.

He tensed and slid his gun from his shoulder holster, wondering if he was overreacting.

The kitchen door burst open. Griff dived to the floor and rolled under the kitchen table. When he reached the other side, he shot at the intruder, a man wearing a ski mask. The guy fell backward, but returned fire.

Griff had aimed to wound, hoping he could cuff the guy to make him talk. Then he heard glass breaking in the living room, and his heart leaped into his throat.

There were two of them! The other guy was going after Claire and Jenna!

Griff shot again, and this time the intruder went down and stayed down. Griff scrambled to his feet and rummaged for string. He tied up the assailant and then ran for the stairs.

When he heard the sound of gunfire from above, he found himself praying—for the first time since Helen died—that God would keep Jenna and Claire safe.

# SIX

Jenna heard the sound of gunfire followed by the crash of shattering glass and reacted without thinking, grabbing her weapon and roughly shaking Claire awake.

"Huh?" Claire mumbled sleepily.

"Under the bed," she whispered urgently. She practically shoved Claire to the floor before scrambling across the bed to crouch on the other side, staying low so she could use the edge of the mattress for protection. Her pulse skyrocketed as adrenaline surged through her bloodstream and she hoped and prayed Griff was all right.

Thudding footsteps rapidly ascending the stairs had her gripping the weapon tightly as she waited for the intruder.

The footsteps paused just outside the door, and the minute it banged open she fired two quick rounds. The masked man stumbled backward but managed to return fire. She ducked, grateful his aim went high and wide to the right.

Jenna poked her head up again, grimly taking in the scene. The gunman was lying on the hallway floor, struggling to sit up.

"Police! Hands where I can see them!" she shouted, not daring to approach.

The gunman didn't comply, instead finding the strength to raise his weapon and turn it toward her. She didn't want to kill him, yet any hesitation could be costly.

It wasn't just her life at stake, but Claire's, too.

"Put the gun down," she shouted. A booted foot came out of nowhere, kicking the gun out of the guy's hands. The man made a low sound, then slumped against the wall.

"Don't move," Griff warned in a low voice, aiming directly at the gunman's chest. His dark gaze swept over the room, piercing her with a look of concern. "Are you okay?"

She gave a jerky nod, relieved beyond belief that he was okay. "Yeah. You?"

He nodded. "Fine. I tied up the other guy downstairs."

She swallowed hard. "Come on out, Claire."

Claire crawled out from under the bed, her thin body shaking as she stayed close to Jenna.

"We need to tie him up and then get out of here," Griff ordered.

Jenna knew he was right. In fact, she could barely fathom that these men had found them at Griff's house in the first place. The guy she'd shot had fallen unconscious, so it wasn't likely they'd get information from him. She grabbed the duffel bag, rooted around for her handcuffs and tossed them to Griff. Then she slung the strap of the duffel over her shoulder.

"Here, put these on," Jenna said, pushing the clothing Claire had taken off earlier into the girl's arms.

Claire quickly complied, pulling on the tattered jeans and yanking the sweatshirt over the long T-shirt she'd slept in. To her credit, she didn't complain as she shoved her feet into her running shoes and then looked up. "I'm ready."

Griff finished cuffing the unconscious gunman. "Stay close," he whispered. "Could be more of them waiting outside."

Jenna nodded, using her hand to push Claire directly behind Griff in an effort to sandwich the girl between them to keep her safe.

Jenna followed Griff's lead, hugging the wall as they made their way downstairs. At the bottom he peeked around the corner, looking into the kitchen, then froze.

"What's wrong?" Jenna whispered.

"The guy I shot is gone," Griff said in a hushed voice.

Jenna's stomach twisted at the implication. The injured man was either not hurt that badly or he'd had help to get free. Time was of the essence. They needed to get far away from

Griff's place. "Maybe we should call for backup," she whispered.

"I'd rather get away from here before he returns to finish us off." Griff stealthily moved through the kitchen, pausing to scoop up his laptop and pass it backward to Jenna.

No one dared break the silence, although Jenna heard Claire's soft gasp as they edged around a small pool of blood on the floor, evidence of the man who'd managed to escape.

A few seconds later, Griff led the way out into the garage. The vehicle was exactly the way they'd left it, but she watched as Griff quickly made sure there was no one hiding inside, even checking the trunk, before he opened the back passenger door.

"Get in and stay down," he whispered.

Claire didn't hesitate to crawl into the back, crouching low on the floor behind the driver's seat. Jenna rounded the vehicle to get in on the passenger side.

Griff slid behind the wheel and jammed the key into the ignition as Jenna put on her seat belt and opened the passenger-side window. "Be ready for gunfire," he warned. He jabbed the button on the visor to open the garage door and at the same time twisted the key to start the car.

The minute the door was open wide enough, he hit the gas, causing the vehicle to shoot out of the garage. Jenna clung to the door handle with her left hand while keeping her gun trained through the window with her right hand.

She was braced for the worst, but thankfully there was no sound of gunfire echoing through the stillness of the night. Although she could hear the distant sound of police sirens.

"We're safe for now. Should we call it in?" she asked Griff as he drove away from the scene of the crime.

"I'm sure one of the neighbors reported the sound of gunfire," he said without taking his eyes off the road.

She frowned. "Shouldn't we go back and meet up with them?"

Griff let out a heavy sigh. "Yeah, but I'm not willing to take the risk, not with a gunman on the loose. I refuse to put your life and Claire's in the line of fire."

Jenna's jaw dropped in shock, and she forced herself to close it with a snap. Until the past few days, Griff never broke the rules. He'd even reprimanded her and Nate for not following protocol on the Brookmont case.

She knew he hoped to be the deputy chief of operations one day, and leaving the scene of a crime involving an officer shooting was not going to help.

"Why don't you drop me and Claire off somewhere and head back?" she suggested. "Leaving like this is only going to risk your career."

This time when he glanced at her, she saw the angst reflected in his dark eyes. "Do you really think I'm the kind of man who would risk your life and Claire's for the sake of some stupid promotion?"

She stared at him in surprise. She was about to point out that he was doing the same thing she and Nate had done a few months earlier, when she heard the sound of muffled sobs.

"Claire?" She closed her window and tucked her weapon away. "What is it? What's wrong?"

"I—I almost g-got you both k-killed," she said between gulping sobs. "I—I'm sorry."

"Shh, it's okay," Jenna said in a soothing voice. "This isn't your fault."

"She's right, Claire," Griff said in a gruff tone. "If anyone's at fault, it's me."

"You?" Jenna shook her head. "Hardly."

"Oh, yeah?" Griff challenged. "Then how did they find us at my place?"

She stared at him as a shiver snaked down her spine. He was right. How had the gunmen found them? "We got rid of Claire's phone," she murmured.

Griff pulled over to the side of the road and turned in his seat to face her. "This car," he said. "I left it parked on the road near the front of your house. We were inside for a while before I left. Maybe those guys put some sort of tracker on it?"

She swallowed hard. "It's possible," she agreed, then spread her hands helplessly. "So, now what?"

Griff scowled. "Now we get a different car."

"Where?" she asked.

"Headquarters. Where else?" he countered. "We'll need to swap this squad for a different one before we head out of town. It's not the best option, but we'll figure out how to get a less conspicuous vehicle later."

Jenna sat back in stunned silence as Griff navigated one side street and then another, heading back toward headquarters. She hated the thought of Griff sacrificing his integrity, his career, for her and Claire.

At the same time, she was humbled by his willingness to stick by her. And she couldn't deny that she was glad to have him there.

Despite her determination not to be a victim, she'd been running from danger for the past twenty-four hours, as had Claire. Jenna was deeply relieved she didn't have to face investigating this mess alone.

Griff fought an internal battle between his duty as a lieutenant for the SWAT team and the instinctive need to get Jenna and Claire someplace safe. It seemed that danger lurked around every corner, and never in his entire career had he been shot at twice in less than a day.

This must be exactly how his deputies had felt when they'd gone off grid to protect innocent lives from an unknown threat. And he hated realizing he'd done a disservice to them by putting reprimands in Nate's and Jenna's personnel files. He made a silent promise to remove them once they'd found a way out of this mess.

In the past few years he'd worked hard to keep his image above reproach, so that no one could claim that he might turn bad, the way his parents had taken to a life of crime.

Yet he knew there was no way he could live with himself if he let something happen to Jenna and Claire.

He could feel Jenna's lingering gaze and forced himself not to squirm in his seat. Yeah, he should go back to the scene of the crime. Both he and Jenna had fired in self-defense. But he knew the protocol would be to confiscate their weapons and put them on desk duty pending the outcome of the investigation. Plus, every officer-involved shooting was now being reviewed by the Criminal Investigative Bureau run by the state. Miles of red tape that would take weeks, if not months, to get through.

No, he couldn't do it. Not when it was clear that Claire was in danger. Not to mention, Jenna's life was on the line, as well. It was amazing they'd got this far without suffering a serious injury.

Griff knew that Jenna had been a huge asset in

keeping Claire safe and taking out the guy who'd got upstairs. As much as he preferred being a loner, he was forced to admit they made a great team.

He switched off the headlights as he approached their headquarters parking lot. He pulled in and parked in the back row, near three other squad cars. After throwing the gearshift into Park, he turned off the engine and glanced at Jenna.

"You and Claire should stay here. I'll go inside to get the keys to another vehicle."

She frowned. "Maybe I should go. The dispatcher has a list of our addresses, so she probably knows she sent officers to your neighborhood."

He drummed his fingers on the top of the steering wheel thoughtfully. "Last night there was a ruckus outside your house, too."

She shrugged. "Yeah, but I still think it will be less noticeable if I go inside to borrow a set of wheels."

Griff didn't like it, but couldn't argue with her logic. He glanced over his shoulder to where Claire sat huddled in the corner of the backseat. "Are you okay staying here with me?"

A ghost of a smile crossed her pale face. "Yes. Without you and Jenna I'd be dead."

She was right, and the truth sat like a rock in the pit of his stomach. Jenna didn't wait, but slid out of the car and hurried across the parking lot, her shoulders hunched against the chill in the air.

It didn't sit well with him to let Jenna go off on her own to pick up the keys to a different squad car. Not that the simple errand held any significant element of physical danger.

But it could harm her reputation. One she'd worked extremely hard to establish.

"Mr.—uh—Lieutenant?"

He glanced back at Claire. "Call me Griff," he suggested in a soft tone. "Are you worried about Jenna? Don't be. She'll be back soon."

"I just wanted to say I'm sorry," Claire whispered. "It's my fault that you and Jenna are in danger. I shouldn't have come here."

"None of this is your fault, Claire. You're safe with us." He paused, then added, "But I'd still like to know how you figured out where Jenna's house was located."

"I was in a coffee shop not far from the hospital when two sheriff's deputies came in. I told them Jenna was expecting me, but that I'd lost her address." She shrugged. "Maybe it was because we look so much alike, but the officers gave me the information."

Griff sighed. No way should those deputies have given Jenna's address to a stranger. What were they thinking? He wanted to give them a stern lecture. "I don't suppose you remember their names?"

Claire hesitated. "I don't want them to get in trouble because of me."

Griff wanted to press the issue, but didn't. After all, the situation had worked out for the best. It was a good thing Claire had found Jenna's house, even if she had inadvertently led the assailant there. Things would have turned out very differently if the attacker had actually found Claire instead. He doubted the girl would have managed to get away.

"Okay, you don't have to tell me their names," he said. "But I need you to promise me something."

"What?"

He pinned her with a grim look. "You need to promise to stay on the straight and narrow from now on. Especially since you're Jenna's younger sister. She's a police officer, and if you decide to break the law, you could tarnish Jenna's reputation, taking her down with you."

There was a long silence. "I promise," Claire finally said. "I don't want to hurt Jenna. And I don't want to be back out on the streets, either. Being taken by Stuart Trent showed me how good I had it with the Bronsons."

It was a tough lesson to learn, that was for sure. "Try not to keep looking backward," he advised, although he knew it was easier said than done. "All you can do is move forward from here."

Claire nodded and lapsed into silence. A few minutes later, Jenna returned with a satisfied expression on her face. "Got them," she said, dangling the keys. "It's just a few parking spaces down from here."

In less than five minutes, they were settled in the new vehicle and heading back toward the highway. He glanced at Jenna. "Where to? The hotel close to church? Or somewhere else?"

Jenna hesitated. "I think we might be better off heading to my grandpa Hank's cabin. It's an hour away, which should give us some time to regroup."

He nodded in agreement. "Tell me how to get there."

Jenna gave him directions, and since it was half-past midnight, there wasn't any traffic bogging them down. Forty-five minutes later, he turned onto a gravel road, bumping over deep ruts as they approached the cabin.

Claire had fallen asleep in the backseat, which he thought was probably a good thing. He and Jenna left her there, unwilling to disturb her rest while they climbed out of the vehicle.

Jenna had taken the flashlight from the glove box. Griff followed her as she went to the edge of the cabin and crouched down, feeling along the wall. He had no idea what she was doing, until she removed a loose chunk of concrete at the base of the cabin and pulled out a key.

Moments later she had the door unlocked and opened. She paused in the doorway, glancing at him. "Give me a minute to flip the switch in the fuse box."

"No problem." He couldn't see much in the darkness, but from what he could tell, the place was rustic, yet surprisingly cozy. Jenna's influence? Most likely.

Two lamps flooded the room with light, and he blinked, giving his eyes a moment to adjust. Jenna returned to the main living area. "It's nothing special, but we won't freeze or starve," she said with some degree of self-consciousness. "The wood-burning stove is the main source of heat, so I'll get a fire started. There are two bedrooms. Claire and I will take the one with the twin beds."

"It's perfect for what we need," he assured her. "I'll go wake up Claire."

She nodded and crossed to the stove. Since Jenna knew how the contraption worked better than he did, he left her to the task and headed back outside.

Claire was propped against the door, so he opened the opposite side and knelt on the seat, reaching out to shake her. "Claire? We're at the cabin."

Claire startled badly, letting out a screech and shrinking away from his touch. He mentally kicked himself for scaring the poor kid.

"I'm sorry," he said, wincing when Jenna rushed outside to see what was wrong. "I didn't mean to frighten you."

Claire stared at him for a moment before she relaxed with a sigh. "Not your fault," she said. She ran a shaky hand through her hair and pushed open the door she'd been sleeping against.

They walked inside. Jenna took one look at Claire, then joined them, frowning with concern. "We're safe here, Claire," she said, putting her arm around the teen's slim shoulders.

Griff scrubbed his hands over his face, wishing he could really believe that. But he'd thought they were safe at his house, too.

He'd been wrong.

Worse, one of the gunmen had managed to get away.

Jenna showed Claire the bedroom where they'd stay for the night, leaving him to take over making the fire. Soon he had a nice blaze going.

He sat back on his heels, staring at the flames for a long minute before closing the stove door. As he rose to his feet, Jenna returned.

"Is she okay?" he asked.

Jenna rubbed her hands over her arms, her expression troubled. "I think so. She's been holding up surprisingly well, considering what she's been through in the past few days."

"Yeah, that's for sure." Griff stayed where he

was, even though he really wanted nothing more than to pull Jenna into his arms. He didn't understand exactly how it had happened, but somehow Jenna had got under his skin.

"I keep thinking about how different our lives would have been if we'd grown up together," Jenna said with a frown. "My childhood was no picnic, yet I somehow ended up in a better place than Claire."

The stark expression in her eyes was too much to bear. He took a step closer, unable to resist offering some measure of comfort. "It's not your fault, Jenna. Aren't you the one who believes God has a plan? That even if we don't know what it is, we're supposed to have faith and trust in Him?"

She stared up at him for a long second, hope and joy shimmering from her eyes. And, somehow, he found himself leaning forward, as if instinctively needing to kiss her.

Jenna moved closer, as though meeting him halfway. Then she abruptly stopped and pulled back.

"Good night," she muttered hastily. Before he could move, she spun around and vanished into the bedroom she'd share with Claire.

Leaving him to stand there in frustration, even though he knew Jenna was off-limits. Not just because they worked together, but because she deserved someone better. Not a guy who was partly responsible for his wife's death.

Right now, he needed to keep his head in the game and concentrate on keeping them all safe— not wonder what Jenna's mouth would taste like if he kissed her.

# SEVEN

Jenna fumbled in the darkness, trying not to wake Claire. She couldn't believe she'd come within a nanosecond of kissing Griff.

Her boss.

The man who'd risked everything to keep her and Claire safe.

At some point, she'd stopped seeing Griff as just her superior. Instead, he'd become a partner. Someone she worked in tandem with.

A man she could trust. At least professionally.

But not personally, she reminded herself. She knew better than to trust her instincts when it came to personal relationships. She picked the wrong men, which meant Griff was wrong, too.

The bed smelled a little musty, but she did her best to ignore it. She tucked her weapon under her pillow and took several deep breaths, hoping to find a way to relax.

They were safe at Grandpa Hank's cabin, but the past twenty-four hours had been difficult, at best. Claire had brought danger with her, although she certainly hadn't asked to be re-adopted. Thankfully Claire was safe now.

Her sister. Oh, sure, Jenna didn't want to believe she'd been adopted by her parents, but every time she looked at Claire, she knew the truth. They obviously shared the same blood. And Jenna was glad that God had looked out for Claire, giving her the strength to get away from Stuart Trent.

Jenna didn't sleep well that night, and the minute dawn peeked over the horizon, she slid out of bed and padded to the main room, shivering in the cold. After feeding more wood into the stove, she headed to the kitchen to see what food, if any, her grandpa Hank had left behind.

Good thing she found a box of instant oatmeal, along with cans of soup and beef stew, more than enough to hold them over for the next day or so. She filled the teakettle with water and set it on top of the small electric stove.

While waiting for the water to boil, Jenna made a pot of coffee. She stared out the window at the wooded area surrounding the cabin, remembering the summer days she'd spent here with her grandpa. Her only real father figure had taught her how to shoot a gun, surprised and pleased every time she hit her mark.

She'd loved her mother, but living with her abusive father hadn't been easy. Moving in with her grandfather and spending her summers in the cabin had been her salvation. Jenna wished that Claire could have had the same opportunity.

The creak of a floorboard made her glance over her shoulder to find Griff standing behind her. "Didn't mean to startle you," he said in a low, gravelly voice.

"You didn't. Hope you like instant oatmeal. That's about all we have as far as breakfast food."

"Sounds good to me." Griff scrubbed his hands over the rough bristles covering his cheeks. "Is that coffee?"

"Help yourself," she said with a wave of her hand. Ridiculous to notice how ruggedly handsome he looked, even when he wasn't clean-shaven as he normally was at work. She tore her gaze away with an effort.

"Ahhh, hits the spot," Griff murmured, sipping from a cracked mug.

She couldn't help but smile. "I know, right? I'm not sure how Claire manages without it."

Griff raised a brow. "You think that because you're sisters she should like coffee as much as you do?"

"Maybe," she said with a shrug. She opened the packets of oatmeal and dumped the dried oats into three bowls.

"You share other mannerisms," he pointed out.

"Really?" She hadn't noticed anything of the sort. "Like what?"

"When you talk it's hard to tell your voices apart and you both use your hands a lot for emphasis. And then there's the way you both pinch the bridge of your nose when you're trying to concentrate."

"Hmm." She couldn't deny his observation, although it would take some time for her to become accustomed to having a sibling. The matching bracelets and their resemblance were impossible to ignore. She changed the subject. "We need to come up with a game plan. I know you have your laptop, but I don't think we're going to find much in the way of internet access up here."

He grimaced. "I was afraid of that. I know you wanted to attend church today, but afterward we need to pay a little visit to the Bronsons'."

She was touched by Griff's willingness to take her to church services. But was it worth the risk? "I don't think it's a good idea to go to church. At least a few of the guys from the team will be there with their families, and it might be better to keep a low profile. Word about the gunshot victim we left behind at your place will spread like wildfire. We need to stay off grid."

Griff frowned. "Are you sure you're okay with skipping service?"

Did they really have a choice? Probably not. "I'm sure. I'll read the Bible for a bit instead."

He looked surprised by her statement, but before he could say anything, the teakettle whistled. She jerked at the noise, then carefully set her coffee mug down so she could pour the hot water into the bowls.

Griff leaned over to help her stir the mixture, far too close for comfort. Thankfully, Claire trudged into the kitchen a few minutes later.

"Something smells good," she said, in lieu of a greeting.

Jenna glanced at her, glad to see the distressed expression had disappeared from her eyes. "Good morning."

Claire slipped into a chair and picked up a spoon, but Jenna stopped her with a hand on her arm. "Wait—we need to pray first."

Her sister glanced up at her in surprise. "Really?"

"Really." Jenna sat beside Claire, then waited for Griff to settle in across from her. She bowed her head. "Dear Lord, thank You for providing this food we are about to eat and for watching over us the past few days, keeping us safe in Your care. Amen."

"Amen," Griff echoed.

Claire grimaced. "I hope you're not going to get all preachy on me," she muttered.

Jenna raised a brow at her sister's tone. "Don't you think that maybe God had something to do with bringing us together? That His hand helped keep us alive over the past twenty-four hours?"

Claire flushed and shrugged. "I guess you could be right. Sorry."

Jenna didn't push the issue, knowing that Claire had been through a lot over these past few days. And it wasn't her fault that she'd been raised without faith.

When her phone rang, Jenna scowled, recognizing the number on the screen. "It's someone at headquarters," she said, pushing the button to ignore the call.

Seconds later, Griff's phone rang. He looked grim as he, too, ignored the call. "Turn off your phone and take out the battery," he suggested.

She followed his lead, knowing it was for the best. The caller could have been someone from the SWAT team, or it could have been their boss. Either way, they were better off on their own.

"Claire, I need directions to your adoptive parents' house," Griff said, effectively switching the conversation to the next step. "We're going to head over there later this morning."

Claire frowned but nodded. "Okay, but I'm warning you, they won't be happy to see me."

Jenna scowled. "That makes us even, because I can guarantee they won't be happy to see us, either. Especially when we point out that their little re-adoption trick was illegal."

Claire stared at her, as if surprised by the vehemence in her tone.

"We don't know that for sure yet," Griff

pointed out. "Could be that they were careful to make it legal."

He was right. Private adoptions could be legal, but she felt for certain that what had happened to Claire after the so-called re-adoption wasn't. "We'll see."

When they finished their meal, Griff stood and carried his empty bowl to the small stainless-steel sink. "Claire and I will clean up the dishes if you want to read."

She was touched he'd remembered. "All right, thanks." Jenna could hear Griff and Claire speaking as she slipped into the bedroom, and she found she was glad that her sister wasn't afraid of Griff anymore.

The Bible was in the top drawer of the nightstand located between the twin beds. She pulled it out and opened to her favorite passage, the Twenty-Third Psalm.

*The Lord is my shepherd, I lack nothing. He makes me lie down in green pastures, He leads me beside quiet waters, He refreshes my soul.*

Reading the familiar words filled her with a sense of peace. How many nights had she read this while living in Ruth's shelter? How many nights did she pray that her father wouldn't be set free?

Too many to count.

Her father was free now, and she could only pray that God would continue to protect her.

Jenna wished Claire could find the same sense of satisfaction from faith as she had. Griff, too, for that matter. She didn't know the details surrounding his wife's untimely death, but they all knew he'd taken it hard.

She could certainly understand. But Griff also needed to be able to move forward with his life. So she made a silent promise to help them both find their way to God.

Once the dishes were washed, dried and put away, Griff tried to get more information from Claire. First he had her write down the address and basic directions to get to the Bronsons'. Then he asked more questions about everything she remembered about the night she'd escaped from Stuart Trent.

"I told Jenna everything I know," Claire protested in distress.

"Please bear with me," Griff said gently. "You mentioned other girls, including the one who gave you a penknife. How many girls, total?"

"Four," Claire said softly.

"And you're certain they were given drugs?" he pressed.

She nodded and pinched the bridge of her nose, the same way Jenna did. "They all had the same glazed look in their eyes, the one my mom had when she was using. And I saw needles and syringes in the bedroom. I remember wondering if there was a way I could use the needle to escape."

Griff wished he didn't have to make her relive the horror she'd experienced, but there might be something buried deep in her memory that could help them. "Did you hear any of their names?"

She lifted a slender shoulder. "Just first names. Abby, Carol, Shaunee and Brenda." She lifted her dull blue gaze to meet his. "Shaunee is the one who slipped me the penknife."

"Why do you think she did that?" he asked. "Seems like she would have used it to try and get away herself."

Claire shook her head helplessly. "I don't know for sure, but I got the impression that once they were hooked on drugs, they didn't want to leave anymore. Maybe she thought it would be easier for me to break free before I was given anything."

He hated to admit that there was some logic in what she said. "And how many other men were there?"

"Just the two of them, Stuart and the other guy. Stuart helped the other guy take the four girls away, then came back by himself, so that's when I attacked him." She licked her lips nervously. "I hope you don't arrest me for that."

"Claire, there's no way you'll get arrested for fighting to get away from those men. Please trust me on this."

She tried to smile. "Okay. Jenna said I needed to trust you, so I will."

He was glad Jenna had put in a good word for him. "I'm glad. Is there anything else you can remember? Any other names? Maybe the street name where the apartment was located?"

She frowned for a moment before letting out a heavy sigh. "I'm sorry. I was so scared, so determined to get far away from the place that I don't even remember looking at street signs. I'm sure I'll recognize it when I see it, though."

Griff sat back in his seat. "That's fine, Claire. Thanks for trying."

"Do you think we'll ever be able to find the other girls?" Claire asked in a plaintive tone.

He hesitated, then decided he needed to be honest with her. "I don't know, but I can assure you that's our goal. First we have to find the guys who took you. Once we do that, we'll be one step closer to finding the girls."

"I hope we can find them," Claire said. "It's not fair they're stuck in that terrible life while I managed to get away."

"I know." He reached over to squeeze her hand. "Try not to think about it too much," he advised.

"It's hard not to," Claire admitted. "I'm glad I managed to get away, yet sad that they're still doing whatever the men order them to do."

He hesitated, unsure what to tell her. If Jenna

were here, she'd encourage Claire to lean on faith. He'd attended church growing up, but not in the past few years.

Especially not since Helen died. Since his inattentive driving and their heated argument had contributed to that fateful crash.

"Prayer helps heal all wounds," Jenna said from the doorway. "I think if you give God and prayer a chance, you'll find some semblance of peace."

Claire looked skeptical, but nodded, obviously unwilling to antagonize her sister. "Okay, I'll try."

"Good. Griff, we should probably get going soon, since we're about an hour outside of Milwaukee."

"It feels a bit early to be knocking at elderly people's doors," he said, glancing at his watch. "But maybe we can take the computer with us and stop someplace that offers free Wi-Fi. We also need to pick up new phones."

"Okay. We should grab groceries, too," Jenna added. "There's only canned goods for the rest of our meals."

Normally he wouldn't be too concerned about when his next meal might be, but Claire deserved better. She still looked gaunt, as if a stiff breeze would flatten her.

"Okay, let's hit the road. What about the fire? Do we need to put it out?"

"I'll close off the damper," Jenna explained. "Lack of oxygen will cause the fire to go out."

She looked comfortable roughing it in the cabin, and he was struck once again by how different Jenna was from Helen. His wife wouldn't have been caught dead in a place as rustic as this.

Or, if she was forced to stay, would certainly not be smiling about it.

He shook off the troubling thoughts, knowing that no matter how much he liked and admired Jenna, there was no way he could even contemplate some sort of relationship with her. He needed to stay away from temptation.

That near kiss couldn't happen again.

Within five minutes they had the cabin locked up tight and were once again driving down the bumpy driveway toward the highway. They stopped at the first big-box store that he saw and waited in the parking lot for it to open.

"Phones first, groceries later," he said. Jenna nodded in agreement, leading the way to the electronics section. They picked out new phones, including one for Claire, then sat for a few minutes to charge them using the car charger and activate them. When they were ready, Griff ditched their old phones in the Dumpster behind the store.

"Next stop, the Bronsons'," he said, heading back to the interstate. Griff turned the radio dial to a news station, anxious to know what was being said about the injured man he'd left behind in his house.

It didn't take long to hear his name mentioned as a person of interest.

*Lieutenant Griffin Vaughn is believed to have shot at two intruders who entered his home last night. One of the victims has escaped, but the other is listed in critical but stable condition in the ICU. Lieutenant Griffin Vaughn and Deputy Jenna Reed are both being asked to turn themselves in for questioning.*

Jenna turned to look at him, her gaze troubled. "That explains the phone calls. Maybe you should go in," she said softly. "I can easily protect Claire in the cabin."

He shook his head. "I'm not going in without you, and you know what the protocol is in a police shooting. They'll take our badges and guns, then stick us on desk duty."

"I know, but I hate knowing that you're in trouble because of me," Jenna insisted.

"No, that's not true. You're both in trouble because of me," Claire corrected her with a sigh.

Griff turned the radio off with a flick of his wrist. He figured they had about twenty-four hours before his boss put APBs out on them. "Never mind—we'll just stay the course, okay? Confronting the Bronsons should give us something concrete to work with."

Jenna looked as if she wanted to argue, but

then sat back with a sigh. "I really don't know why you're sticking your neck out for me," she said softly. "You have a lot to lose, Griff."

He shrugged, but didn't answer. What could he say when he wasn't exactly sure why he was doing this, either? All he knew for sure was that he wasn't going to leave the two sisters to face this on their own.

They stopped at a café that boasted free Wi-Fi, and he used the computer to finish searching for information on Stuart Trent. An hour later, they were on the road again, heading for the Bronsons'.

"There—on the right, the third house from the corner," Claire pointed out. "White siding and black trim."

The place looked innocuous enough, but Griff remained on high alert as he pulled over to the curb right in front. There was a moment of silence before Jenna pushed her door open with more force than was necessary.

He glanced back at Claire. "Are you ready?"

Claire shook her head. "I'd rather stay here."

He exchanged a questioning look with Jenna, who shook her head. "Too dangerous. You don't have to say anything to them, Claire. We'll do all the talking."

Griff kept Claire sandwiched between him and Jenna as they approached the front porch of the Bronsons'. Jenna rapped sharply on the door. She had her badge out and didn't hesitate to flash it the moment the door opened.

"Claire?" a shaky older voice asked. "Is that you?"

Jenna scowled. "My name is Deputy Reed and this is Lieutenant Vaughn. And I'm sure you remember Claire. We have a few questions for you and your husband."

The woman peered at them in confusion, and Griff couldn't help thinking that his grandmother had looked younger than this woman before she'd passed away. "You can't bring Claire back. She doesn't live here anymore," Judy Bronson said with a frown.

"Don't worry. We have no intention of leaving Claire with you," Jenna said, her tone ringing with disdain.

"Ma'am, if you don't mind, we really need to ask you about Claire's adoption," Griff said in a stern tone. "Do you still have the paperwork you were given by Mr. Stuart Trent?"

"Uh, I think so." Mrs. Bronson hesitated, then opened the door wider and shuffled into the living room. "Bob? The police are here. They want to see the paperwork from Claire's adoption."

Every muscle in Jenna's lean frame was tense with suppressed anger, so Griff put a reassuring hand on the small of her back. "Easy," he murmured. "Let's get what we came for before you let them have it."

She twisted around to glance at him, and he despised the sheer anguish in her eyes. "I wish we could arrest them," she whispered fiercely. "They act like they don't even care about Claire's welfare."

"Because they don't," Claire said in a dull tone.

"Shh," he cautioned. "We need them to co-operate."

"Eh? Paperwork? Where did you put it?" An older man's voice groused from the other room. "Check the desk."

"I found it," Mrs. Bronson said, returning to the living room. "Here." She thrust the papers at Jenna, studiously avoiding Claire's eyes. "I don't know why you're here. It's all legal. I assume she's in trouble again?"

He didn't think it was possible, but Jenna's spine stiffened. "No thanks to you," she said curtly. "This poor girl was almost drugged and sold on the streets, but hey, if everything is legal then there's nothing to worry about, right?"

"What are you talking about?" Judy Bronson said, taking a step back in horror. "Mr. and Mrs. Trent were a very nice young couple, more capable of handling Claire than we were."

Griff took the papers from Jenna, fearing she'd crush them into unrecognizable pieces if he didn't. "How did you find Mr. Trent?" he asked.

Judy blanched. "I—we— Bob? Bob! They're asking how we found Mr. Trent!"

"That's none of your cotton-pickin' business," the older gentleman snapped as he clomped into the room. "You have the papers you asked for. Now git out."

Griff felt Jenna lunge forward and he grabbed her arm in the nick of time. "Let's go," he said. "They're not worth it."

Jenna didn't move, her laser gaze centered on the couple. "If we're able to prove this so-called adoption is as illegal as we suspect, I'll be back to arrest you both."

"A-arrest us?" Bob Bronson stuttered, his face going ruby red. "For what?"

"You put a young girl's life at risk because you were too tired to work on being good parents." Jenna practically spit the words at them. "You should be ashamed of yourselves."

Griff couldn't help but admire Jenna's fiercely loyal attitude, but he gently tugged on her arm, anxious to review the paperwork. "Let's go."

Claire clung to Jenna's side as he led them back outside. They were about halfway to the squad car when he heard the loud crack of a gunshot.

"Get down," he shouted, pushing Jenna and Claire mercilessly to the ground and covering their bodies as much as possible with his.

# EIGHT

Jenna was squashed between Griff and Claire, barely able to breathe, much less pull together a coherent thought. She couldn't believe someone was shooting at them! Griff's weight abruptly shifted to the side, giving her the ability to draw in a shaky breath. She eased off her sister, too.

"Are you all right?" she whispered to Claire.

The girl nodded, her eyes wide with fear.

"We need to get to the car," Griff whispered. "Claire, stay close."

Jenna pushed Claire over to her left side, estimating from the sounds that the shots had come from the right. She showed Claire how to belly crawl toward the car.

When they reached the relative safety of the squad car, Jenna pulled open the back passenger door, gesturing for Claire to get in first. "Keep your head down," she commanded.

She glanced back at Griff, who had managed to hang on to the paperwork they'd taken from the Bronsons. He caught up to her and paused, listening intently. Jenna swept her gaze around the area. The place seemed unnaturally calm. Quiet. As if the neighbors were shut up in their respective homes, peeking fearfully from behind heavy curtains.

"Get inside," Griff said, his face a grim mask of anger. "We need to get out of here."

"What about the Bronsons?" Claire asked in a hoarse whisper. "Are they in danger?"

"I don't think so," Jenna murmured reassuringly. Ironic that Claire was worried about them, when they'd made it clear they didn't want anything to do with the girl who had lived under their roof for five years. "The shooters are after us, not them."

"They'll be fine," Griff added. "No doubt they're calling 911 right now."

Jenna climbed into the backseat beside Claire. She made her way over to the opposite side of the car and then slowly peeked up enough to see through the window.

There wasn't any sign of the shooter, although that didn't necessarily surprise her. The shot had sounded as if it came from a rifle, not a handgun. No doubt the gunman was perched high in a tree branch or maybe on the roof of one of the houses across the street.

Jenna hated knowing that she'd somehow dragged Griff into this mess, right into the center of danger. She glanced back at where he was still crouched outside the vehicle. "I'm going to slide into the driver's seat," she whispered.

"I'll drive. Just give me a minute to make sure the coast is clear," he responded.

"If they want Claire alive, he may confuse me for her and hold off on shooting," Jenna insisted. "I'd rather you stay in the backseat, protecting Claire."

Without waiting to see if Griff did as she'd asked, Jenna wiggled through the opening between the front bucket seats. She was shorter than Griff, so keeping her head low wasn't too difficult.

"Please," Claire begged. "Let's get out of here."

Griff capitulated, making his way into the backseat. He tossed Jenna the keys. "Be careful."

Jenna waited until Griff was safely inside before she slipped the keys into the ignition and cranked the engine to life. Keeping her head down as low as possible while still being able to see, she hit the gas and pulled away from the curb.

She held her breath as she drove, turning right at the corner, desperate to put distance between their car and the shooter. Her arms were tense, braced for the sound of another gunshot, hoping, praying, the bullet wouldn't find its mark.

It was a good ten minutes before she edged into an upright position. Still, she gripped the steering wheel with tight fingers until they reached the interstate.

"H-how did they find us?" Claire asked, breaking the thick silence.

"Good question. We weren't followed," Griff said in a gruff tone. "I made sure of that."

"I know we weren't," Jenna agreed. "I was keeping an eye out, too. But think about it for a minute. If Stuart Trent is part of the human-trafficking ring, then it's not a stretch to think he had someone staked out at the Bronsons', anticipating that we may show up."

"I led us into a trap," Griff muttered, his tone full of self-recrimination.

"I didn't consider the possibility, either," Jenna felt compelled to point out. "I figured we'd be safe enough in the bright light of day."

"We're going to need another vehicle," Griff said in a weary tone. "There's a chance the shooter may have gotten the license-plate number."

Jenna pondered that for a moment. "So what if they do have it?" she asked. "The car is registered to the Milwaukee County Sheriff's Office, not to either one of us personally. Besides, they already know where we live. So as long as we don't return to either of our homes, we should be fine. They can't very well track us by the plate number alone. Not unless they have someone within law enforcement at their disposal. From the way things have played out over the past few days, that doesn't seem to be the case."

Griff was silent for a long moment. "You may be right," he agreed. "There isn't any evidence they have dirty cops working for them. Judging by the direction the shots came from, and the fact that we were only inside for a few minutes, it's not likely they planted a tracking device on the vehicle. But we need to check, to make sure. I'd still rather get a less-noticeable car."

"Sounds good." Jenna concentrated on the highway stretching before her. "I'll pull over at the next rest stop so we can check the car. Then what? Should we head back to my grandpa Hank's cabin?"

"Yeah, but we have to be extra careful to make sure we're not being followed. I still don't like the fact that they might have our license-plate number. And we know our boss is looking for us, too."

Jenna thought for a moment. "We can take the added precaution of smearing mud over the license plates. We can double back, then take less-known roads to get to the cabin."

In the rearview mirror she could see the corner of his mouth tip up in a smile. "I like the way you think, Jenna."

She smiled back at him, knowing it was ridiculous to be pleased by his offhand compliment. Why did she care so much what Griff thought of her? She knew she was a good cop. An excellent sniper.

A woman.

No way. She reeled in her wayward thoughts. The last thing she needed was for Griff to start thinking of her as a female instead of a colleague. She couldn't afford to let something like the magnetic pull she'd experienced last night, when she'd almost kissed him, catch her off guard again.

No matter how different he was from Eric and Aaron Simms.

No matter how much she liked him.

She focused on getting off at the next rest stop and pulling into a parking space far away from the other vehicles. Jenna pushed open her door and climbed out of the car, subtly stretching her sore muscles. The past twenty-four hours had resulted in more bruises and soreness than she'd experienced since those torturous months in the police academy.

"Are you okay?" Griff asked in a low voice, his brow pulled together in a frown.

"Of course," she said, abruptly dropping her arms to her sides. She waved a hand, brushing off his concern in an effort to keep her distance. As if the musky scent of his aftershave hadn't permeated the inside of the car.

She turned away and crouched beside the car. Griff joined her, and between the two of them they made sure there were no tracking devices. Then she went over to find some mud, smearing it across the license plate. When finished, she headed inside to wash up.

Upon her return, she noticed that Claire and Griff were deep in conversation outside the car. As she approached, she overheard Griff asking questions about the Bronsons.

"I told you they were glad to see me go," Claire muttered in a dejected tone. "But it's my own fault. I kept breaking their rules and got into a lot of trouble, to the point of being arrested."

"It's not your fault at all," Jenna protested hotly, growing angry all over again at how horribly the Bronsons had treated her sister. "They had no right to just give up on you."

Claire shrugged, and her attempt at a smile didn't reach her blue eyes. Eyes that looked very much like Jenna's own. "It doesn't matter now. I'm safe with you. With both of you," Claire added, including Griff. "I wish you could find and arrest those men, though, before they hurt anyone else. I'll never forgive myself if either of you get hurt because of me."

"We'll find them," Griff assured her gruffly. "When we get to the cabin, we'll review what we know, go through the paperwork the Bronsons gave us and decide our next steps."

"Absolutely." Jenna arched a brow at Griff. "I suppose you want to drive?"

He winced. "It's nothing personal," he protested. "But, yeah, if you don't mind, I'd rather drive."

She rolled her eyes, but fished the keys out of the front pocket of her jeans. "Here you go," she said, tossing them in the air.

Griff caught them easily and flashed her a wide grin before climbing into the driver's seat. "Thanks, Jenna."

His smile rocked her back on her heels, and she battled back a wave of attraction.

*Do. Not. Go. There.*

Yet saying the words with emphasis and actually finding a way to act on them were two different things.

She slid into the passenger seat and latched her seat belt. Claire did the same. Griff backed out of the parking spot and headed onto the highway. But he took the next exit and went north instead of west.

"Did you look at the paperwork the Bronsons gave us?" she asked.

"Not yet. We should wait until we get to the cabin."

He was probably right. After all, seeing the terms of the agreement between the Bronsons and Stuart Trent in black and white was likely to fill her with rage all over again.

She didn't normally have an issue with reining in her temper, but for some reason, she'd found it exceedingly difficult to hold herself together in the older couple's home. Obviously, they had no idea what kind of person they'd turned Claire over to or what Stuart Trent's plans for Claire entailed. But they also made it clear they weren't interested in having Claire back.

Which was fine with her, since she had no intention of allowing Claire to return.

Jenna took a deep breath, then let it out slowly. No sense in wasting her time thinking about the Bronsons. Despite Claire's concern that Trent might go after them, she doubted he'd call attention to himself by doing that. What good would it do?

Abruptly, she reached out to grab Griff's arm. "What if we're wrong? What if Stuart Trent does go after the Bronsons to keep them from testifying against him?"

"Calm down. We're a long way from anyone testifying against anyone," Griff said.

Jenna couldn't quite ignore the rock that sat in the pit of her stomach. "I know, but still. They staked out the house and waited for us. The Bronsons really could be in danger."

"I knew it," Claire muttered from the backseat. "We should have made them come with us."

"Listen, there's no reason to jump to conclusions," Griff said firmly. "I'm sure someone called the police when they heard the gunfire. Their neighborhood is probably crawling with cops. And I'm convinced the shooter took off and is long gone by now."

Jenna grimaced and nodded. "You're right. I'm sorry," she added, glancing back at Claire. "I shouldn't have overreacted like that."

"I just…" Claire's voice trailed off. Jenna wanted to kick herself when she noticed the sheen of tears in her sister's eyes. "I don't want to be the one responsible for them getting hurt."

"You aren't responsible," Jenna said in a gentle tone. "I don't want them to be hurt, either, but remember that they were the ones who initiated the re-adoption proceedings in the first place, not you."

"But only because I was such a terrible kid," Claire cried before burying her face in her hands.

"Don't cry, Claire. Please don't cry," Jenna said, reaching back to rub Claire's knee, wishing she'd kept her big mouth shut. "We'll call the police in their district and explain why we believe they're in danger. It's going to be okay, Claire."

Claire struggled to get her emotions under control and eventually swiped the tears from her face.

"We'll pray for them, okay?" Jenna closed her eyes. "Dear Lord, please keep Bob and Judy Bronson safe in Your care. Please give us the strength and guidance we need to arrest the people responsible for these crimes. Amen."

"Amen," Claire whispered.

"Amen," Griff echoed.

Jenna added a silent prayer that Claire would also find the peace of mind she deserved. And when she glanced over at Griff, she was humbled and amazed to find that he was looking at her with approval.

Something she liked a little too much.

"Use your new phone to call the police," Griff suggested. He was very glad they'd already purchased the devices and taken the time to get them charged and ready to go.

He knew Claire was listening, too, as Jenna spoke to the dispatcher in the eighth district. "I'd like to speak to a detective," she said.

As Jenna explained their concerns for the Bronsons, he could tell by her tone that the detective needed a bit of convincing. Was it possible that the detective had heard the news and realized who they were? He tensed, expecting the worst, but Jenna quickly ended the call and handed the phone back to him with a sigh.

"They did go out to the scene and found a few slugs but no suspects," she said. "They promised to keep an eye on the Bronsons."

"The detective didn't say anything else? He didn't recognize your name from the news?"

"No, he didn't. Maybe word hasn't gotten around yet."

"Thanks for making sure the Bronsons are safe, Jenna," Claire murmured.

Jenna's mouth drooped in a frown, and Griff knew she was still feeling bad for getting Claire upset in the first place. But looking back over the events, he couldn't honestly say he'd do anything differently. Going back inside for the Bronsons would have been too dangerous, and besides, he firmly believed that they were the intended targets, not the Bronsons.

Did the shooter even know Jenna was a cop? The guy who'd burst into her bedroom knew, as she'd identified herself as one, but according to the news station, they had him in custody.

The shooter was growing bolder. More reckless. Which only made Griff hope that he'd make another mistake. Sooner, rather than later.

The emotional avalanche had worn Claire out, and even Jenna seemed quieter than normal over the next half hour.

Griff was relieved when they were within a few miles of Jenna's grandfather's cabin. As he passed a large sign boasting fast-food choices, he realized it had been hours since their breakfast of instant oatmeal.

"Anyone hungry?" he asked, breaking the silence. "There are a few places here where we could pick up something for lunch."

Claire brightened at the mention of food. "Fried chicken?" she asked hopefully.

He glanced at Jenna, who nodded. "Sure. Why not?"

"Sounds good." He pulled into the parking lot. Within fifteen minutes he was back with a bucket of chicken and a container of mashed potatoes. He handed the bag over to Jenna before sliding in behind the wheel.

The mouthwatering scent of deep-fried chicken permeated the interior of the car, making him realize just how hungry he was.

"Mmm, my favorite," Claire said with appreciation.

"Really?" Jenna said with a smile.

Claire ducked her head and shrugged. "I know it probably seems silly, but eating out was a rare treat. There wasn't a lot of money to spare for frivolousness."

Jenna nodded, but didn't say anything more. A few miles later, Griff slowed down to turn into the gravel driveway, the car bouncing over the ruts as he slowly edged toward the cabin. When he came to a stop, Jenna was the first one out of the car, heading over to unlock the door.

By the time he and Claire made it inside, Jenna was stoking the fire in the wood-burning stove. The interior of the cabin was cool, but Griff knew the small place would warm up quickly enough.

Jenna had set the food on the kitchen table, and Claire hurried over to pull out plates and silverware. Jenna washed her hands, then joined them at the table.

Griff waited for Jenna to start the prayer, but Claire was the one who spoke up first. "Dear Lord, thank You for this food we are about to eat. We also thank You for keeping us safe from harm today. Amen."

"Amen," he and Jenna said simultaneously, making Claire laugh.

The mood lightened as they ate, and it was clear that Claire enjoyed every bite of the spicy chicken. It wasn't until they'd finished the simple meal that Griff remembered the forms the Bronsons had given them.

"I'll be right back," he said, excusing himself from the table. "I forgot the paperwork in the car."

"No problem. We'll clean things up here," Jenna offered.

He nodded and hurried outside to retrieve the documents. They were badly wrinkled, and he smoothed them out against his thigh before carrying them inside.

He settled down at the kitchen table and spread them out so he could place them in the proper order. The documents were full of legalese, making them difficult to understand.

The first page talked about the adoption agreement between Stuart and Debra Trent and the Bronsons.

The logo in the upper right-hand corner looked familiar, but he couldn't quite place it. He scanned the document, flipping the pages until he reached the final signature page.

The attorney's name at the bottom of the document stopped him cold.

Darnell Franklin.

His gut churned and he swallowed hard. Darnell Franklin was one of the partners of Linden, Henley and Franklin, LLP.

The same law firm where his wife, Helen, had worked, from the time she graduated from law school to the time she died.

# NINE

Jenna finished washing the dirty dishes at the sink and glanced over at Griff with a frown. He'd been sitting motionless, staring at the adoption agreement.

Claire was still drying the dishes and putting them away, so Jenna crossed to where Griff was sitting.

"What is it?" she asked in a low voice, hoping Claire wouldn't hear.

He shook his head slowly, then cleared his throat. "I've met this guy, this lawyer, Darnell Franklin. I can't believe he was the one involved with Claire's adoption."

A shiver rippled down her spine. "So the adoption was legal?"

"I'm not sure," Griff admitted, letting his breath out in a heavy sigh. "I don't know what to think. Franklin's a partner in a big law firm. Why would they be involved in something sketchy like re-adoptions?"

"Money?" Jenna suggested drily. She frowned, sensing there was something more bothering Griff. "When did you meet him?"

His deep brown eyes met hers, his expression troubled. "At one of the firm's parties my wife, Helen, insisted we attend."

She caught her breath as realization dawned. "Your wife worked for him?"

His head bobbed in a jerky nod. "Yeah."

Jenna whistled softly. "I'm sorry," she murmured, even though she wasn't exactly sure why she was apologizing. She hadn't known Griff's wife. Rumor had it that she'd been killed shortly before Griff had brought her onto the SWAT team. A car crash. Griff had been driving. She imagined that was one of the reasons he'd taken her death so hard. He probably felt guilty and likely still loved her.

A fact that she'd do well to remember.

"What did you find out?" Claire asked as she came over to join them at the table.

"A lead on the attorney who did the adoption," Jenna said quickly.

"Oh." Claire looked disappointed. "I guess it was legal."

"Not necessarily," Griff said in a grim tone. "The entire thing bears investigating. At least we have a place to start. I think we should pay a visit to Darnell Franklin."

Jenna doubted the attorney would admit to

doing anything remotely illegal, but they didn't have too many other leads, so she nodded. "When? It's just after one o'clock on a Sunday afternoon. It's not likely he's in the office."

Griff grimaced. "You're right. Even if we call first thing in the morning, we'll be fortunate to get an appointment the same day. Since Darnell happens to be one of the partners at the law firm, I doubt he'll see us if we don't go through proper channels."

Jenna silently agreed and couldn't deny being knocked off kilter at the thought that the attorney who'd handled Claire's re-adoption was one of the firm's partners. And why would a partner stoop to doing something that was likely illegal?

"How long ago did your wife work there?" she asked, trying to fit the pieces together.

Griff grimaced. "She started there right after law school, which would have been roughly five years ago. And she stayed until her death two years ago."

Claire's second adoption had been recent, less than a few weeks ago. But what if Claire's wasn't the first re-adoption? What if Darnell had been willing to do whatever it took to make partner? "I wonder if he was a partner when your wife worked there."

"We can look that up online, but I seem to remember he was," Griff said.

Jenna frowned. "We need some sort of cover

story to meet with him. Won't he remember you from the party you attended with your wife?"

Griff looked thoughtful for a minute. "If he remembers meeting me at the party, he'll know I'm a cop. But if I tell him that I want to talk to him about Helen's death, he might agree to see us."

"Why on earth would he think you'd talk to him about Helen's death?" Jenna didn't understand Griff's logic. "Surely your insurance company already settled the case. There's nothing to file a lawsuit over, is there?"

Griff shrugged. "I can pretend that I uncovered additional information about the driver of the other vehicle and that I'm seeking legal advice about whether I can file a wrongful-death lawsuit. Hopefully that's enough to get us an appointment."

"Maybe," she hedged.

"What about me?" Claire asked. "What am I going to do while you meet with the lawyer?"

"You'll either come with us or stay behind with me," Jenna assured her. "We're not leaving you alone." The memory of how close they'd come to losing Claire earlier that day still bothered her. Although it also didn't escape her notice that the shooter seemed to be aiming at Griff, rather than Claire.

"Did you meet the lawyer during the adoption process?" Griff asked. "Will he remember you?"

"No, I didn't meet him. The Bronsons worked

everything out with the Trents." Claire's tone held a note of bitterness. "What I wanted didn't matter much."

Jenna put her arm around Claire's shoulders. "It's all over now," she reminded the girl. "We just wanted to be sure that if Franklin sees you, it won't blow our cover story."

Claire shrugged and stepped away from Jenna. "It won't. Let me know when we're leaving again." Claire tossed the dishrag on the counter and walked into the bedroom, shutting the door behind her.

Jenna sighed, knowing her sister was still bothered by the fact that she'd got away when the other four girls hadn't. Not that Jenna could blame her. What Claire had suffered had been bad enough, but those poor girls were probably in worse shape by now.

What if Shaunee hadn't given Claire the knife? Claire would have been given drugs and forced into a life of prostitution and addiction.

The very idea made Jenna feel sick to her stomach.

"I need some air," Griff muttered, spinning on his heel and heading back outside. She watched as he let himself out of the cabin and closed the front door behind him. She wanted to follow him but stayed where she was, not at all certain he desired company.

But when the seconds stretched into minutes,

she couldn't fight the urge to check on him. When she couldn't stand it a moment more, she rose to her feet and slipped outside.

Dark clouds had moved in, bringing the threat of a storm. She hesitated, seeing Griff standing over to the left side of the porch, staring off into the woods.

She approached cautiously. "Hey, are you all right?"

He turned his head to look at her over his shoulder. "I'm not sure," he admitted in a low voice. "I keep thinking about the law firm where Helen worked, wondering why they'd do anything even slightly illegal."

Her heart ached for him. "I doubt it was the entire firm," she pointed out. "If Darnell is involved, it's likely he acted on his own."

"Possibly," he said, in a tone laced with doubt. "But what if Helen knew? I can't stop thinking that it's possible she was involved in something illegal, too."

"Don't, Griff," Jenna pleaded, placing her hand on his arm. "Don't let this mess tarnish your memories of your wife. It's not fair to her, since she can't very well defend herself, and it's not fair to you, either. There's no sense in looking for trouble where there isn't any."

Griff reached up and covered her hand with his, sending a shiver of awareness down her spine that she ruthlessly shoved away. The poor guy was grieving for his wife. She had no business thinking about how much she liked him as a man.

A mentor.

A friend.

"We were arguing that day," Griff said softly. "I wish I could go back in time to erase the fact that we were fighting mere seconds before the crash."

It was on the tip of her tongue to ask what they were fighting about, but she managed to hold the question back, knowing the details were none of her business. "It's better to remember the good times."

Griff's hand tightened over hers. "There weren't as many good times as I would have liked," he admitted roughly. "We didn't see much of each other the last year of our marriage."

Jenna was surprised by his admission. "Well, I'm sure your schedules were crazy, especially if you were working second shift and she was working primarily during the day."

He let out a bitter laugh. "She worked well into the evening most days. And went in to work even on my days off. Including weekends."

"Sounds like she was putting in a lot of hours," Jenna conceded with a wince. "But I imagine that most new lawyers have to work similar hours. At least, that's the way it's portrayed in books and movies."

"Yeah." Griff kept his hand over hers for a long moment before releasing her. He turned to face her, and she wished she could read the enigmatic expression in his eyes as he stared down at her. "Unfortunately, this mess seems to be a little too similar to that movie where the young lawyer stumbles across the partner's criminal activities."

She hated hearing the frustrated anger in his tone. "You don't know that," she said again. "Helen probably didn't know anything about what Darnell was doing."

"I hope not," he said in a choked tone. "I honestly can't stand the thought that she might have been involved."

The ravaged expression on his face tugged at her heartstrings, and Jenna found herself stepping forward and slipping her arms around his waist in a reassuring hug. Right now, they weren't boss and subordinate, but friends who needed to support each other.

His arms wrapped around her, holding her close, and he surprised her by resting his cheek against her hair. She closed her eyes, his unique male scent going straight to her head, making her pulse jump erratically.

She told herself that Griff needed a friend, nothing more, but when his hand stroked her back and he pressed a kiss against her temple, all rational thought vanished from her mind quicker than a hummingbird taking flight.

She wasn't exactly sure how it happened, but he lifted her chin with his finger and lowered his mouth to hers—tentatively, at first, as if asking permission. Then, when she offered absolutely no resistance, he deepened the kiss.

For several moments she reveled in Griff's embrace, so different from what she'd experienced with Eric. An abrupt flash of lightning followed by a crack of thunder made her jump, flooding her mind with a healthy dose of common sense.

She broke away from his kiss, berating herself for being a fool. Not only was Griff her boss, but they'd just been discussing his deceased wife and his feelings of guilt over her death.

Her legs felt weak, so she rested her forehead on his chest, willing her pulse rate to return to normal, even as the thundering beat of his heart reassured her that he wasn't unaffected by their kiss, either.

"I better go inside," she offered lamely, forcing herself to pull away from the sheltering warmth of his arms.

Griff didn't say anything or try to stop her as she turned and made her way back into the cabin.

Her fingers trembled as she stoked the fire in the stove. The interior of the cabin seemed small. Cozy. Far too intimate. They should leave, go back to find a restaurant that offered free internet access.

But just then the sky opened up, torrential rain coming down hard on the roof of the cabin. Glancing outside, she noticed that the ruts in the driveway were quickly filling with water, creating a muddy terrain.

Impossible to leave now.

But she needed something to do. Something to keep her from thinking about Griff. Getting involved with her boss would only lead to heartbreak. She needed to keep her distance.

Before it was too late.

Griff stayed out on the front porch of the cabin, reliving the incredible kiss he'd shared with Jenna, not wanting to go back inside even when the thunderstorm hit with a vengeance.

He must have lost his mind. That was the only logical explanation. He'd lost his marbles and, now that he'd tasted the sweetness of Jenna's mouth, knew that going back to being just friends and colleagues wouldn't be easy.

Not impossible, but definitely not simple.

He took a deep breath and told himself that he was only imagining Jenna's kiss was better than anything he'd shared with Helen. He and Helen had once been in love.

The fact that their marriage had been on a rocky path for the year before she'd died didn't mean it was all bad. Early in their marriage they'd seemed to want the same things. But toward the end they couldn't have been on more opposite paths.

Enough, he told himself sternly. Picking apart every nuance of his last weeks with Helen wouldn't get him anywhere. Jenna was right about the fact that he shouldn't let the news of Darnell's signature on Claire's adoption papers tarnish his view of his wife. Helen knew he was a cop. The last thing she would have done was allow herself to get involved in something shady.

But, then again, he couldn't deny that Helen's attitude had changed that last year. She'd insisted on going to Chicago to shop at the most elite stores, where a dress cost half his paycheck. She'd asserted that image was important and that she needed to dress for success in order for people to believe in her abilities as a lawyer. Personally, he'd liked her best wearing jeans with her dark hair gathered up in a ponytail rather than twisted into the fancy French braid she'd worn to the office.

He gave himself a mental shake, knowing that a desire for fancy clothes and a luxurious lifestyle was a far cry from being involved in something illegal. He desperately wanted to believe Helen hadn't turned greedy, the way his parents had.

If only he could prove it.

Moving quietly, Griff let himself back into the cabin, lingering for a few minutes in the warmth radiating off the wood-burning stove. He glanced over to where Jenna was seated at the kitchen table, peering intently at Claire's adoption paperwork.

She was so beautiful, and her strawberry scent still clung to his skin from holding her in his arms. He had no business kissing a woman who reported to him, a woman he didn't deserve. He swallowed hard and forced himself to act as if nothing had happened.

"Are you interested in coffee?" he asked. "It's going to be a while before we can head into town."

"Absolutely," Jenna said, lifting her head to meet his gaze. Her smile was wry. "The storm is making me want to crawl into bed and sleep the afternoon away."

"Yeah, I know what you mean." He filled the carafe with water.

"It's driving me crazy not having anything to do," Jenna said on a sigh.

He leaned against the counter, crossing his arms over his chest and waiting for the coffee to finish brewing. "We need to come up with a strategy," he said. "I've been thinking. There are several boxes of Helen's paperwork from her home office stored in my attic. Maybe we can sneak back into my place to get them."

"Not sure going back to the scene of the crime is a good idea," Jenna argued. "There's probably at least one officer stationed there."

He knew it was a long shot. "We can create some sort of diversion, at least long enough for me to slip inside."

Jenna looked thoughtful. "I'd rather sneak into Franklin's office."

Why hadn't he thought of that? He abruptly dug in his pocket for his keys. Sure enough, he still had the spare key Helen had given him. "Maybe we can," he said, holding it up.

Jenna's eyes widened, but then she frowned. "What are the chances that Darnell didn't change the locks after Helen died?"

"Fifty-fifty," he said with a shrug. "Higher if Helen didn't mention she made a spare set for me."

"Why did she?" Jenna asked as he poured two steaming mugs of coffee. He carried them over to the table and took a seat across from her, out of touching distance.

"In the first few months of her job, she misplaced her keys. She went nuts trying to find them, not wanting to look foolish to her new boss. We eventually found them, but Helen decided to make a second set, just in case." He stared at the key ring. "I should have thought of this earlier."

"The key will get us into the building, but it may not get us into his office," Jenna pointed out.

"Yeah, but once we're inside, I'm betting we can use a credit card or a lock pick to get in." The more Griff thought about the possibility of searching Darnell's office, the more motivated he became.

"Look, the rain is already lightening up," Jenna pointed out. He glanced through the window, noting the rain had stopped as abruptly as it had started. "What do you think? Should we risk trying to get out of the driveway?"

He lifted a brow. "Might be pushing it," he said slowly. "But I'm willing to try. I'd rather be doing something constructive than sitting here, twiddling our thumbs."

"I agree." Jenna shot a worried glance toward the closed bedroom door. "I'm concerned about Claire, though. She was pretty upset after the shooting incident earlier today."

"So much for promising her we'd keep her safe," he muttered harshly.

Jenna eyed him over the rim of her mug. "There's still time for you to call your boss," she said.

"Not going to happen." Jenna's concern for his welfare was touching, but definitely misplaced.

Claire opened the bedroom door and walked into the kitchen. "Are you going to get in trouble for shooting the man at Griff's house? The guy who's now at the hospital?" she asked.

"I hope not," Jenna said honestly.

"They tried to kill us first. We'll be fine," Griff said firmly. "Besides, I thought we agreed that we're in this together."

Jenna flashed him a wry smile. "Right."

"So now what?" Claire asked. "Are we heading out to find internet access?"

"Not until we know for sure we won't get stuck in the driveway," Griff said. From what he could tell, the ground had absorbed some of the standing water, but there was still plenty of mud to make finding traction difficult. Maybe using Jenna's grandfather's cabin wasn't the smartest move.

"I have an idea," Jenna said, leaping to her feet. "There's some lumber stacked in the back of the cabin. If we put the boards down across the mud, we should get enough traction under the tires to get out."

"Great idea."

Two long sweaty hours later, Griff drove carefully down the driveway, nearly getting stuck twice before managing to reach the road.

Jenna filled Claire in on their plan to search Darnell's office. The teen didn't say much about it, although Griff could tell that she was a bit apprehensive as they headed into Milwaukee.

"The offer of going to the shelter is still open,"

he said, capturing Claire's gaze in the rearview mirror. "You'd be safe there."

"I'm sticking with you," Claire insisted.

The rain had morphed into a light drizzle. He parked the car, then turned to Jenna. "Wait here while I see if the key works."

She nodded in agreement. He ducked his head as he strode up to the front of the building, trying to make it look as if he belonged there. There was no sign of any security cameras, which surprised him.

He slid the key into the lock and twisted it. There was a distinctive click as the door opened. Turning back to look over his shoulder, he gestured for Jenna and Claire to come forward.

Within seconds they crossed the threshold and were inside the plush office suite. There was a large lobby area along with several offices. Griff stood for a moment, waiting for his eyes to adjust to the dimness of the interior. The dark clouds outside provided good coverage, but they also hid any natural light. He flipped the switch on the flashlight app on his cell phone.

"Which one is Darnell's office?" Jenna asked in a whisper.

He flashed his light on the wall, noting the nameplate mounted to the right of the door. He moved down the row of offices until he found the one with Darnell's name outside the door.

"Now what?" Jenna asked.

He paused, trying to think of a way to break into the guy's office undetected. From this point forward, they had to tread carefully.

The last thing they needed was to give Darnell any hint that they were onto him.

# TEN

The office area was impressive, but Jenna could only look at the fancy furnishings and wonder if re-adoptions had helped pay for the dark wood desk, soft carpet and sleek oil paintings adorning the walls.

One potentially illegal adoption could be explained away as a mistake, but if Darnell had brokered several, as she suspected, he must have known he was breaking the law.

The idea that he'd willingly gone along with putting teenage girls, or other children, in harm's way made her sick to her stomach.

Unfortunately, they couldn't arrest the guy based on her gut feelings. They needed proof. The adoption papers they'd taken from the Bronsons' were a good start, but certainly not enough.

Which was exactly why they were here. To find something more to go on. Anything to give them a hint as to where to find the other girls.

Griff wrapped his hand in the fabric of his

sweatshirt and tried the door handle. Of course it was locked.

"Maybe we should leave," Claire said in a shaky voice reeking of uncertainty. "We can't break the lock. He'll know we were here."

Jenna flashed her sister a reassuring smile. "Don't worry. We're not going to damage anything."

Griff pulled out his wallet and extracted a thin card. He glanced back at Jenna. "I need you to hold the light so I can see. This will take two hands."

"I didn't think the credit-card trick worked very well," Jenna said. She took the phone from his hand and held the device at an angle so the beam of light illuminated the door handle.

He shrugged. "It's a long shot, but we've come this far."

Since he was right, she didn't say anything more. Sliding the card into the narrow crack between the door and the frame, he jiggled the card in an attempt to pop the lock open.

Griff persisted with a patient diligence that she couldn't help but admire. She would have given up after the first few attempts, but he continued to work at the joint between the door and the frame again and again.

Jenna swallowed a wave of frustration. She glanced around the spacious reception area, wondering if it would be easier to pry into the receptionist's desk to search for keys.

Suddenly there was a loud click and the door opened. Claire gasped in surprise and Jenna put a hand on Griff's shoulder, aware of the warmth seeping through the fleece to singe her fingers. She quickly moved backward, putting distance between them. "Nice job."

"Don't touch anything with your bare hands," Griff warned as they eased into Darnell's personal office space.

Jenna returned his phone, then pulled hers out to use as a flashlight. She moved cautiously, trying to avoid getting too close to the windows that lined the wall. She turned toward the huge desk, and the beam of light bounced over a picture of Darnell standing between two teenage boys. His kids, she presumed, and he was likely divorced since there wasn't a photograph of his wife anywhere to be seen.

"I hate him for what he did to me," Claire whispered beside her, staring at the photograph in horror.

*Hate* was a strong word, but Jenna understood where her sister was coming from. Claire had been one of the fortunate ones, managing to escape. But how many others hadn't?

"Let's concentrate on finding evidence," she suggested, trying to divert Claire's attention from the photograph. She wanted to encourage her sister to forgive, the way Jesus taught them to, but this obviously wasn't the time.

"The desk drawers are locked, too," Griff said with regret. "Unfortunately, the credit-card trick won't work on these types of locks."

Jenna didn't want to leave empty-handed. Meeting in person with Darnell wouldn't give them the information they really needed. She moved the light over the top of the desk, then frowned. "Wait a minute. Are these files?"

"Where?" Griff asked eagerly.

"Here." The top of the desk was covered by a leather calendar holder, but along the left-hand edge she could see evidence of something hidden underneath. She shone her light on the area and Griff nodded with satisfaction.

"Easy," he said, using the edge of his sweatshirt to lift the leather calendar holder up, revealing two files. "No fingerprints, remember?"

Jenna nodded, using her elbow to move the files off of each other. "Here's one labeled *Theresa Porchanski*."

"Porchanski?" he echoed with a frown. He carefully flipped open the file. A photograph of a scowling teenage girl with red hair and freckles stared up at them.

"Another re-adoption?" she whispered, lifting her gaze to Griff's.

"Maybe," he agreed grimly. "That name seems familiar to me, although I can't remember where

I heard it." He leaned closer as if trying to read the details listed on the paperwork.

"No!" Claire grabbed Jenna's arm with a fierce grip. "We can't let him hurt more girls!"

"Shh, it's okay," Jenna said, putting her arm around Claire's waist. Her sister leaned heavily against her and Jenna knew the teen was reaching her breaking point.

"Jenna's right, Claire. This is exactly what we're looking for," Griff said in a soothing voice. "Evidence that may help us find these girls. I won't bother setting up a meeting with him now that we have the file."

Lightning momentarily brightened the sky, clearly visible through the large windows. A loud crack of thunder made them all jump. Jenna glanced at her watch, realizing with surprise that they'd been inside the building for almost a full hour.

"We need to get out of here soon," she murmured. "We don't want anyone to report seeing a light in here."

"Agreed. I think it's best if we make copies of this file to take with us," Griff said, "leaving the original where we found it."

That plan worked for her. "I'll hold the light. You take pictures with your phone."

Moving the papers without touching them wasn't easy, but they managed to copy the entire file before putting it back the way they'd found it. Then they turned their attention to the second file. That one wasn't related to any type of adoption, but appeared to be divorce proceedings.

"Should we copy this, too?" she asked Griff.

He hesitated, then shook his head. "No. I can't imagine that has anything to do with the missing girls."

Jenna hesitated then shrugged. "You're probably right." She lifted the edge of the leather calendar holder high enough that Griff could slide the two files back where they'd found them.

Jenna wished they could have found more files, especially ones related to Claire or any of the other girls, like Shaunee.

She turned away from the desk, struggling to understand how adoptions and divorces brought in enough money to pay for such a swanky office.

Then again, he could charge whatever he wanted if the adoptions weren't exactly legal.

Claire pulled herself together as they left the interior of Darnell's office. Griff made sure the door was locked behind them.

Jenna could feel the tension radiating from Claire's body as they walked back outside, ducking their heads against the new onslaught of rain. Once they were inside the car, Griff cranked the heat in an effort to warm them up and dry their damp clothing.

"Where are we going?" Jenna asked, as Griff drove away from the office building.

"I think it's best if we find a motel nearby to spend the night," he said.

"Grandpa Hank's cabin is safer," she argued.

"Not exactly. We barely managed to get out of the driveway, but that's not the real issue. We need internet access so we can do a search on Theresa Porchanski."

Jenna sighed. "You're right—a motel makes sense. But we need to choose a place that the sheriff's department hasn't used before." She pulled out her phone and began to search. "Here's a place, The Quilted Bee Motel. They claim to have internet access in every room."

"Sounds perfect."

She provided Griff with directions, then sat back in her seat, trying to ignore the sense of dread that seeped into her bones.

Staying in a motel wasn't dangerous. But it was just nine hours ago that they'd heard the news about being wanted for questioning. How much longer would they be able to avoid being tracked down by their deputy chief?

She glanced at Griff's handsome profile, and it was on the tip of her tongue to remind him that it would be best for both of their careers if they simply turned themselves in.

Yet she couldn't help thinking that if they did that, they'd miss their chance to save Theresa Porchanski from the same fate Claire had nearly suffered.

Her gut hardened with resolve. No, they couldn't turn themselves in. Not yet. Not until they had more evidence.

So she closed her eyes and prayed for God's strength and support, and that they were on the right path, doing the right thing.

For Claire's sake, as well as their own.

Jenna couldn't live with herself if they allowed Stuart Trent and Darnell Franklin to get away with their human-trafficking scheme.

Those two men, along with any others involved, needed to be brought to justice.

The parking lot of The Quilted Bee Motel was mostly deserted, which was a good thing, in Griff's opinion. It was a single-story building, and while most of the rooms faced the road, there were a few in the rear, as well. Perfect for keeping the squad car out of sight.

"Stay here. I'll be back in a few minutes," Griff said, turning off the engine and pushing the driver's-side door open.

"Tell them we want a room in the back," Jenna said.

He grinned. "You read my mind."

Inside the lobby, an older woman was seated behind the counter, actually working on a quilt.

Apparently the name wasn't just a gimmick. The woman obviously took her quilting seriously.

"Good evening," he greeted her warmly, pulling his badge out and setting it on the counter. "I'd like connecting rooms in the back, please, for me, my partner and our witness. And I need to pay with cash."

The woman's eyes rounded in surprise, then narrowed with suspicion. "Who's going to pay for damages if whoever you're hiding from finds you?"

He had to give her credit for thinking ahead. "Tell you what. I'll give you my credit-card number to pay for damages, but would ask that you don't put it through the system."

She stared at the credit card for several long moments. "What if the card is maxed out?"

"It's not." He tried to think of a way to convince her. "Take down my badge number, too, and if anything happens you can call Chief Deputy of Operations Herbert Markham. I promise you our office will pay for any damages."

"Fine," she grudgingly agreed. She wrote down his badge number and the credit-card information, including the security code on the back, then accepted cash for the two rooms.

"Rooms nine and eleven are in the back," she said, handing over magnetic key cards. "There's a free breakfast here in the lobby if you're interested."

"Thanks." Griff took the keys, then headed

back outside. After sliding in behind the wheel, he handed the key for room nine to Jenna and kept the one for room eleven.

He parked off to the side of the parking lot, near a large oak tree, away from their specific rooms. After tucking his computer under his arm, he followed Jenna and Claire into the motel.

"Keep the connecting door open, okay?" Griff asked, using his key to access his room.

"Sure." Jenna and Claire disappeared inside, and he did the same, setting the computer on the small table before unlocking and opening the connecting door.

Where had he heard the name Theresa Porchanski? His thoughts whirled as he turned on the laptop. The last name, in particular, was familiar to him. And not very common, either.

Searching for Theresa Porchanski wasn't easy. Surprisingly, the girl didn't have a criminal record, the way Claire did. Griff pulled out his phone to review the files. He wished they had printing capabilities and wondered if the quilting lady would allow him to connect his computer to her printer.

Jenna opened the connecting door on her side and he could hear the sound of the television coming from their room. She stood there, the serious expression on her face making him frown. "What is it? Something wrong?"

"Claire turned on the news. There's a reporter

on scene at Trinity Medical Center, where the guy I shot at your place is being treated."

Griff rose to his feet and followed her into the adjoining room. Claire was sitting on the bed, her back against the headboard, hugging a pillow to her chest in a way that made her seem incredibly young.

The journalist finished reporting the prisoner's serious but stable condition before the commercial break.

"I was thinking that it might be good to talk to the perp," Jenna said. "Investigating the girl in the file will prove that Franklin is involved in the scheme, but how is that going to help us find the place where Claire was held?"

"They'll have a cop stationed outside the door," Griff said, considering the idea. "And they want us for questioning, so we can't just stroll in asking to interview the prisoner."

"We could ask Shane for help," Jenna suggested. "Gabby might even be his doctor of record. We know she was at the hospital this weekend."

"Maybe," Griff said, silently admitting that Jenna's idea had merit. "Although I hate dragging Gabby—or Shane, for that matter—into this mess."

There was a long moment of silence before Jenna spoke up. "You have to know that Shane, or any of the guys on the team, would do anything for you, Griff. No questions asked."

He was touched by her level of certainty, but at the same time, that was part of the problem. "I don't want to drag them down with us. It's bad enough that you're involved, Jenna."

"You have it backwards," she said lightly. "I'm the one who pulled you into this. Claire is my sister and I'm going to find the man who assaulted her."

"Me, too," he assured her. "Okay, I'll contact Shane. But I'm not sure he or Gabby can really help. For all we know, this guy is a prisoner of the Milwaukee Police Department, not our Sheriff's Office."

"Shane used to work at MPD, though, so maybe he still has connections," Jenna said. "I think it's worth a shot."

Griff pulled out his phone and then looked at Jenna wryly. "I'm so used to having my contact list to make calls, I haven't memorized the number. Do you know it by heart?"

"Yes, because his number and Nate's are both similar to my old number." She rattled off the digits and he punched them into the new disposable phone. The call went to voice mail, which wasn't too surprising, since Shane wouldn't recognize the number. Griff left a quick message asking Shane to return his call.

He went back to his room to continue his computer search. Less than five minutes later, his phone rang. Warily, Griff answered. "Vaughn."

"Griff? Where have you been? We've been worried about you and Jenna. What happened?"

"It's a long story, and right now I need a favor." Griff didn't want to waste time getting into long explanations.

"Let me guess—car and cash, right?"

Griff had to smile. "Yeah, those two items would be good, but what I really need to know is which district is guarding the prisoner patient at Trinity."

"We are," Shane responded. "The Sheriff's Office. Why?"

Griff couldn't believe things were finally going their way. "Perfect. Can you find out who's on duty tonight?"

"Sure thing. Give me a few minutes and I'll call you back."

Griff ended the call, and at that moment, he remembered where he'd heard the name Porchanski. Only it wasn't Theresa, but Andrea. Andrea Porchanski was a young girl who was part of a child-custody case his wife, Helen, had worked on shortly before she died.

A cold chill snaked down his spine and he pushed away from the computer. The name had to be a coincidence. Helen couldn't have been involved in something like re-adoptions.

But what if she had been?

What if Helen had allowed herself to participate in something illegal, the same way his parents had all those years ago?

# ELEVEN

The news station droned on about the recent surge of crime in the area, but Jenna wasn't really paying attention. She was listening intently for Griff's phone to ring, indicating Shane was returning his call.

Jenna knew that Griff took his leadership role seriously. And while she understood his reluctance to get the rest of the team involved, it was clear they couldn't do this alone. Especially since it probably wouldn't take long before the deputy chief of operations got serious about tracking them down.

A new vehicle would help, but it was still only a matter of time.

"Jenna?" Claire's tentative voice penetrated her thoughts.

She turned to face her sister. "What's wrong?"

"Isn't there something we can do to help that girl? The one whose picture we found in that lawyer's office?"

Jenna felt bad about the obvious distress in the teen's eyes. Maybe she should have pushed the issue of Claire staying at the shelter. Ruth would make room if she called in a favor. "We're working the case," Jenna reminded her. "And to be honest, we don't know for sure that girl is in danger."

"She is," Claire insisted. "I know it."

Since she was probably right, Jenna tried a different tack. "We're going to do everything possible to find her and any other girls who might be in danger, too. Questioning the prisoner patient is a good place to start."

"What can I do?" Claire asked.

"Pray," Jenna answered. When Claire rolled her eyes in obvious annoyance, Jenna reined in her temper. "Don't underestimate the power of prayer. God is always there for us, no matter what. He forgives us our sins and helps guide us on the right path. I lean on my faith whenever times get tough."

"What do you know about tough times?" Claire asked in a rare flash of anger.

Jenna hesitated, then realized she hadn't told Claire about her abusive father. "My mother never told me I was adopted, but I have to be honest with you. I'm glad, very glad, that the man who raised me isn't my real father."

Claire's gaze searched hers. "Why? Did he treat you badly?"

"He focused his anger on my mother at first, and we always had to be worried about what his mood might be when he came home from work. But as I grew older, he began taking his anger out on me, too."

"I'm sorry, Jenna," Claire said, moving closer. "How did you and your mom get away?"

"One night, he almost killed us," she said in a flat tone. "At first, my mother took the beating as if she really believed she deserved it, but when I jumped in to protect her, fighting against him with all my strength, she suddenly began doing the same thing. I think he was shocked, but then he became enraged and hit us even harder. I kept screaming at the top of my lungs, hoping that someone would hear. He grabbed a knife and tried to stab me, but a female police officer barged through the door to save us. Since he was caught with the knife in his hand, I knew he'd go to jail."

"I was wrong. I guess you do know what it's like," Claire said softly, resting her head against Jenna's shoulder.

"I had a concussion and a broken arm. My mother had worse injuries, including a stab wound. We stayed in Ruth's shelter until he was convicted of attempted murder."

"And you became the female officer you admired," Claire added with an insight that surprised Jenna.

"Yes, I did."

"And you really believe prayer helped you get through that?"

Jenna shook her head. "Not at first. I didn't really learn about God and faith until we lived at the shelter. But since then, yes, I do believe. Being a cop isn't easy. We put ourselves in danger almost every day."

"I don't like thinking about it," Claire confessed.

Jenna gave herself a mental head slap. She was trying to soothe her sister's fears, not make them worse. "I'm a trained police officer. Trust me, I know what I'm doing. But I believe God is watching over me, too."

Claire drew in a deep breath and then let it out slowly. "Okay, I'll pray for the girls. And for you. But I hope we find something more to go on soon, because I hate knowing they're in danger."

"I don't like it any more than you do," Jenna said. The shrill sound of Griff's phone snagged her attention. "That must be Shane."

Claire lifted her head and gave Jenna a little push. "Go on. I know you want to hear what they're talking about."

Jenna hesitated, then pulled Claire into a tight hug. "You're not alone anymore, okay? I'm here and God is there for you, too. We'll get through this, I promise."

"I love you," Claire whispered, returning her

hug with a ferocity that made her eyes well with tears.

"I love you, too." Jenna pulled away from her sister and swiped at the tears that might betray her before walking over to the connecting doorway.

She was more determined than ever to find those poor girls before it was too late.

"Okay, I've got good news," Shane said when Griff answered the phone.

Griff glanced up to see Jenna hovering in the doorway. He gestured for her to come in. "Shane, I'm going to put you on speaker, okay?"

"Sure thing."

Griff set down his phone and pushed the button. "Go ahead. We could use some good news."

"The prisoner patient is awake, and he's off the ventilator, so he can talk. Gabby is the one who performed surgery to remove the bullet from his upper left chest."

Griff glanced at Jenna's grim expression. "The slug came from Jenna's gun," he said. "She shot him in self-defense."

"You don't have to tell me," Shane protested. "I believe you."

"I really need to get in there to talk to him," Griff said. "We need information, Shane, and we need it ASAP."

"The deputy chief has been in to talk to him

already," Shane informed Griff. "But Markham hasn't told the rest of us anything. Well, except to order us to let him know the minute you made contact with us," Shane amended.

Griff sighed, knowing that he was putting his deputies in a tough spot. "I'd rather you didn't let him know, at least not yet."

"As if I would," Shane countered, a bit of anger seeping into his tone. "As if any of us would. We've been waiting for you or Jenna to contact us. We're on your side, always."

Griff's throat swelled with emotion at the unwavering loyalty of his deputies. "Thanks," he muttered gruffly.

"Who's on guard duty tonight?" Jenna asked.

"That's the other good news. Our newest team member, Jake Matthews, was looking to pick up overtime. He's working until eleven o'clock tonight."

Griff grinned at Jenna. "Excellent. Now I just need a way to get into the prisoner's room without being seen."

"Don't forget we need a vehicle," Jenna added.

"I have that taken care of. Declan's brother-in-law, Bobby, still has that old Dodge of his. Deck has already agreed to loan it to you."

Griff didn't care what make or model they were given as long as it ran. "Sounds good. What time are you thinking?"

There was a brief pause on the other end of

the line. "Let's get you the new vehicle first, and then we can discuss the plan to sneak into the hospital in more detail."

He glanced at Jenna, who shrugged. "May as well. We're not far from the hospital, either way."

"Okay, when can you meet us with Bobby's car?" Griff asked.

"In an hour. Let's say at eight o'clock we'll meet at the parking lot located right off the Brookmont exit ramp. Does that work for you?"

"Sure. We'll see you then." Griff paused, then added, "Thanks, Shane. I owe you."

"Not true," Shane countered. "We're all here to back each other up, remember?"

Griff couldn't argue with that statement, since it was something he preached to his team on a regular basis. "See you in an hour."

"Is it okay if Claire and I ride along?" Jenna asked. "Sitting here is going to drive us crazy."

He couldn't blame them for wanting to stick together. "Sure, but we don't need to leave for a while yet. Let's see if we can get anything off the documents we copied."

Jenna took notes as he pored over the fine print. The forms were listed as pre-adoption paperwork and unfortunately didn't give them as much information as he'd hoped.

"We'd better get going, or we'll be late meeting Shane," Jenna said, tossing her pen onto the desk. "We'll search the internet again later."

In moments they were back in the squad car, hopefully for the last time, heading toward the Brookmont exit ramp. Griff kept a keen eye out for any police cars tailing them now that they were closer to the scene of the crime. He couldn't help thinking about the possibility that Helen was involved in Darnell's re-adoption scheme. He desperately wanted to go back to his house to search through the boxes in the attic where he'd stored most of Helen's things.

If only his house wasn't still a crime scene.

They arrived at the meeting point a few minutes early, and Griff made sure to park the squad car between two large SUVs, hoping to hide in plain sight. Five minutes passed, then ten, without any sign of Shane.

"Shouldn't he be here by now?" Claire asked in a worried tone. "What if something bad happened?"

"Shane would let us know if he couldn't make it," Jenna assured her, glancing at Griff as if seeking confirmation.

"Jenna's right," he agreed calmly. "He'll be here soon enough."

"I don't know how you stand the pressure," Claire muttered under her breath. "I could never be a cop."

"Hey, you're safe with us, remember?" Jenna said, reaching back to touch Claire's knee. "There's nothing to worry about."

"I felt safer at the cabin," Claire admitted. "Far away from civilization."

"There's Shane," Griff pointed out as an old brown Dodge pulled into the parking lot. "Stay here for a few minutes, okay?"

Jenna nodded, so he pushed open the driver's-side door and walked around to the back of the vehicle, waving Shane over. In a few moments, Shane had parked the brown sedan right behind the squad car.

"Sorry I'm late," Shane said as he approached.

"No problem." Griff glanced over as Jenna and Claire joined him. When Shane stared at Claire in shock, obviously noticing the young girl's similarity to Jenna, Griff quickly made the introductions.

"Your sister, huh?" Shane said to Jenna. "Maybe you should fill me in on the whole story. I feel like I've missed a few pages. Or maybe a whole chapter."

Griff gave his deputy the abbreviated version. "We really need something to go on to find Stuart Trent," he finished. "Is Jake ready to help me sneak in tonight?"

Shane nodded. "Yeah. Prisoner's name is Leo Affron and he's located in the surgical intensive-care unit, third floor, room number five, which happens to be right near the side entrance. In talking to Jake, we think it's best to wait until about ten o'clock before going in. Visiting hours will be over by then and it will be close to the change of shift at eleven, so hopefully the staff will be busy enough not to notice you sneaking in."

Almost two hours, Griff thought with a sigh. But since Shane's logic made sense, he nodded in agreement. "Okay, ten o'clock sounds like a plan. Are you sure Jake's okay with this?"

"He's agreed to keep it quiet," Shane said.

Jenna planted her hands on her hips. "I'd like to be there, too."

"We agreed not to leave Claire alone, and three of us going in will be far too noticeable," Griff pointed out.

Jenna fell silent, but he could tell she wasn't happy. She would be even more upset if she knew he was contemplating sneaking into his house, too.

"I brought cash," Shane said, thrusting a wad of money into his hand. "If you need more, let me know."

Griff divided the money and gave half to Jenna before pocketing the rest. "Make sure you get both of our new numbers programmed into your phone. That way you'll know when we're trying to contact you."

"What are they?" When Shane finished plugging in the numbers, he added, "I hope you call when you have more information to go on. We're all ready and willing to help in any way possible."

"I know, and trust me, as soon as we have something solid to go on we'll be in touch," Griff assured him. "Thanks again."

"No problem."

Griff exchanged keys with Shane and then waited for Jenna and Claire to get situated in the Dodge before he slid in behind the wheel. Bobby's car was old, but the engine purred as Griff drove back toward the motel.

Once they were back in their adjoining rooms, Griff returned to the laptop computer.

"Why don't you let me search for a while?" Jenna asked, coming over to stand beside him. "After all, I need something to do while you're gone."

"All right, have at it," he said, getting up so she could sit in his place.

They worked together for an hour, trying different ways to connect Theresa Porchanski with Stuart Trent, but to no avail. It was interesting to note the adoption wasn't listed in the family-court legal proceedings, though. More proof that it was illegal.

Soon it was time to leave for the hospital. Griff poked his head in to check on Claire, but the teen had fallen asleep.

"We'll be fine," Jenna said, although her smile seemed forced.

"I'll be back before you know it," he promised. She stared at him so intently, he had to wonder if she suspected he had other plans. "Call me if something happens."

"Will do." He hated leaving her here in the motel alone, not because he thought they were in any danger, but because somehow he'd got accustomed to working with her as a partner.

Strange, because up until this recent series of events, he'd always preferred working alone. Now he felt almost vulnerable as he headed into the darkness of the night without Jenna by his side.

The drive to the hospital didn't take long, and when he arrived, he was surprised that the hospital security guard readily buzzed him in without asking any questions.

Griff made his way up to the third floor, only to realize the unit was locked down at night. He found the side entrance, which was also locked. In both areas, there was a phone on the wall, indicating that visitors should call before entering.

Announcing himself as the visitor of a prisoner patient wasn't an option, so he waited at the side door for a few minutes, hoping someone might come out, giving him the chance to get in.

His patience was rewarded in less than ten minutes. A doctor came through the doors, barely glancing at Griff as he strode purposefully down the hall, the edges of his lab coat flapping in the breeze. Griff slid inside the unit, then paused to get his bearings. The room numbers were mounted on the walls, and he easily found room number five.

Sure enough, Jake was the deputy on duty, and Griff gave him a nod as he entered the room. "Thanks for doing this."

"Not a problem, although Leo here hasn't been feeling too talkative," Jake said in a low tone.

Griff made his way to the prisoner's bedside, recognizing the guy Jenna shot. "I'm Lieutenant Griff Vaughn, the man whose house you broke into two nights ago. Who sent you?" he asked in a low tone.

Leo's gaze flicked between Jake and Griff. "I'm not talking to the cops without my lawyer," he whispered hoarsely. He rattled his wrist where it was shackled to the bed. "Maybe you should let me loose."

"No chance. A lawyer isn't going to help you much since you tried to kill a cop," Griff pointed out.

Leo licked his lips nervously. "I didn't know she was a cop," he said defensively. "My lawyer is going to help me get out of this since I had no way of knowing she was a cop."

"Really? I was there when she told you she was a cop," Griff said. "And the girl that she was protecting? She's going to testify about the human-trafficking business you're involved with. No lawyer can fix that. Trust me, Leo, you're going away for a long time. Who's going to protect you in prison, huh?"

Leo's eyes widened with apprehension. "You gotta help me! You gotta get me protection in the joint if I agree to talk to you!"

"I'll agree to get you protection, but you have to give me something to go on. Something to help me find the man who abducted Claire. Who sent you?"

"A guy hired us to get the girl, and we goofed up and grabbed the wrong one the first time. So we were told to get them both, but no one said nuthin' about one of them being a cop," Leo whined. "We were instructed to bring them to an apartment building near the Illinois border."

"Give me an address."

"I don't know the address," Leo protested. "We were going to get directions once we had the girls."

"Then I can't help you," Griff said, turning to leave.

"Wait!" Leo called out in a panic. "Trent. The guy who hired us was Stuart Trent."

Griff glanced over his shoulder. "I already knew that much, and his name is no help if I can't find him." He took another step toward the door.

"Okay, okay." Leo was sweating profusely now. "I'll tell you what I know. The four-family apartment building is located on Clayborn Street. I don't know the cross street, but it's on Clayborn a few miles north of the Illinois border. I swear that's all I know!"

Clayborn was a place to start, but at the same time, Griff had no idea just how many four-family apartment buildings there were in that general area.

"Come on. You gotta believe me," Leo pressed, clearly worried about his future in prison.

"Okay, if I find the apartment building on Clayborn, then I'll arrange for protection." Griff nodded at Jake, then slipped out of the room and out the side door of the unit.

Griff hurried outside, relieved to have a clue, no matter how small.

Surely Claire would remember the apartment building she'd escaped from. All they had to do was drive around until she identified it.

Bringing them one step closer to finding and arresting Stuart Trent and anyone else who might be involved.

# TWELVE

Jenna was determined to find something they could use in their investigation. But so far, she'd been unable to get anything on Theresa Porchanski. She sat back in her chair, scowling at the screen.

Why not check on their prisoner patient? She leaned forward and entered his name into the state database.

She smiled grimly when she hit pay dirt.

Leo Affron, age thirty-one, had been in trouble before, most recently for armed robbery and soliciting prostitution. Both crimes were of interest, especially the latter. Interesting to see he'd got off without much jail time. She was wading through the database, searching for the details on the sentencing and hearing, when she stumbled over the name of Leo's attorney.

Darnell Franklin.

She blinked and looked again, in case her

mind was playing tricks on her. But the lawyer's name was there in black and white.

A surge of satisfaction had her leaping to her feet. Their case was starting to come together, the pieces falling into place. Leo broke into Griff's house with an accomplice who was still on the loose, and she believed his mission was to grab her and Claire. Now she had proof that Leo and Darnell knew each other well over a year ago.

Interesting that Darnell had represented Leo, since he didn't advertise himself as a criminal lawyer.

Her instincts had been right. Darnell was involved in the human-trafficking scheme, right up to his scrawny neck. If only they could get a lead on Stuart Trent.

Griff would hopefully get the information they needed from Leo himself. She glanced at her watch, knowing it was useless to worry. Griff would be back soon enough.

This connection between Darnell and Leo was huge. She paced the tiny width of the motel room, too keyed up to relax.

She abruptly stopped in her tracks as a horrible thought popped into her mind. Darnell wouldn't be happy to know Leo had got caught. That he was right now a prisoner of the Milwaukee County Sheriff.

What if Darnell did something drastic to keep Leo from talking?

She struggled to breathe through the tight band across her chest. The connection between Leo and Darnell couldn't be eliminated since it was already part of the public arrest record. Killing Leo wouldn't change that.

Then again, it was entirely possible that Leo would rat out his own mother to save himself.

Jenna placed a quick call to Shane. Thankfully, he immediately picked up.

"Jenna? Is something wrong?"

"Listen, I know Leo Affron is being guarded by our guys, but I'm worried Darnell Franklin will find a way to get to him."

"Who?" Shane asked in confusion.

"The lawyer who brokered Claire's re-adoption, remember? I went on the circuit-court database, and it looks like Darnell was Leo's lawyer a little over a year ago. I'm worried he'll find a way to shut Leo up, permanently."

"Leo's probably talking to Griff right now, so it will already be too late," Shane said with undeniable logic. "There would be no point to killing him."

"Except Darnell doesn't know we're onto him." She began pacing again. "The lawyer might think he has no choice but to eliminate the potential threat."

"What more do you think we need to do?"

Shane asked. "There's already an officer stationed inside his room. There's no way we'd get funding to add deputies."

"Couldn't you warn them to be on alert for any strange personnel? Maybe see if we can keep a running list of staff names for people entering and leaving the room? You know as well as I do that it's not difficult to dress up like a doctor or nurse."

"That's not a bad idea," Shane agreed. "Maybe Gabby can help from her end."

"Thanks. I appreciate you taking the threat seriously." She disconnected the call, feeling better for having taken some action.

The minutes ticked by slowly, and she kept staring at her phone, wondering if Griff had run into some kind of trouble. Although she was sure he'd call if he needed backup.

Wouldn't he?

She dropped back into the seat she'd abandoned earlier and stared at the circuit-court website. It occurred to her that Claire had stopped talking about her mother.

Their mother, Georgina Towne.

Typing in the name didn't take long, and within seconds the woman's criminal history bloomed on the screen, making Jenna wince when she saw the numerous crimes associated primarily with drugs, shoplifting and the occasional prostitution arrest.

No wonder Georgina's parental rights had been severed.

Claire had got into trouble living with the Bronsons, but it was entirely possible that staying with their mother wouldn't have altered her path much. Jenna hoped Claire really did intend to turn her life around. She desperately wanted Claire to graduate from high school, to have the ability to attend college or a technical school. To do whatever Claire wanted to do with her life.

Her sister would have a fighting chance if she lived with Jenna from this point forward. Jenna didn't have any illusions that it would be easy, but with their mother still serving time in jail, there really wasn't any other option.

No doubt Claire would want to visit their mother. The question was whether or not Jenna should go along, as well. She pinched the bridge of her nose, wondering if Georgina would even remember her after all this time. Granted, Claire had mentioned being told she had an older sister, and they did have matching bracelets, likely purchased by their mother. They'd have to wait until they closed the case, but once they'd put all of this behind them, she'd take the trip.

Taking Claire with her.

And Griff? She pulled herself up short. Why on earth would Griff want to come along? Ridiculous. There was no point in thinking about what it might be like to spend time with Griff on a personal level.

Once they put this case behind them, there would be nothing but professionalism between them.

The fact that the thought was infinitely depressing was no one's fault but her own.

A strip of yellow crime-scene tape stretched between the two trees that were in front of his house. Griff drove by slowly, the hood of his sweatshirt pulled over his head to help hide his light hair.

A sheriff's deputy vehicle was sitting at the curb directly across from his front door. He imagined that the deputy chief was hoping Griff would show up so they could drag him in.

He drove past the cop and turned left at the next corner to swing around the back. Surprisingly, there weren't any police cars stationed there.

Griff inwardly debated the wisdom of sneaking inside his home to search through Helen's things. What was the chance that he'd actually find anything useful? Slim to none.

Yet he couldn't seem to leave.

The mere thought that Helen might have willingly gone along with whatever scheme Darnell had cooked up made him feel sick to his stomach. Had she really broken the law, like his parents? When his parents had died in a car crash when he was eight years old, he'd been devastated by their loss.

It wasn't until later, when he was thirteen and working on a genealogy project for school, that he stumbled across the truth. When he confronted his grandmother, she'd admitted that the police believed the crash was intentional, caused by one of the investors who'd lost most of his life's savings.

After their deaths, the full extent of their extortion had been revealed. Whatever money they hadn't spent had been returned. But even knowing that hadn't made him feel much better. For years he'd struggled to understand why his parents would do such a terrible thing.

From that moment on, Griff had been determined to become a police officer. To uphold the law, no matter what. To prove he was nothing like his parents.

Now he was living that nightmare all over again.

Driven by the need to get at the truth about Helen, he pulled over and parked three blocks away from his place, knowing it would be easier to go in on foot. Keeping the hood over his head, he carefully made his way through neighbors' yards, choosing houses with dark windows, indicating either the occupants weren't home or they were already asleep.

When he was near the lot line dividing his yard from the home behind him, he paused and crouched by a small evergreen tree on the neighbor's property.

He swept his gaze over the area, looking for any sign of police presence. There was yellow crime tape cordoning off the backyard, as well, and from what he could tell, the place had been locked up tight.

Pursing his lips, he considered his options. He'd try the door first, but suspected that the place had been secured with padlocks as a crime scene. There was a small basement window that he could probably bust through to get in, but breaking the glass would be noisy. Someone had already boarded up the patio doors, so getting in that way wouldn't work.

There was a window above the kitchen sink, but he decided the basement window was less likely to be noticed. Keeping low, he ran through his backyard and ducked beneath the crime-scene tape. From there, he inched his way toward the basement window.

He tried to open it, but it was locked from the inside, which was what he'd expected. He felt along the edge of the window, trying to find a soft spot on the frame.

Unfortunately, he kept his house in tip-top shape. Which left breaking the glass and hoping that the cop sitting out front wouldn't hear the crash.

Using his elbow, he hit the glass in the corner of the window, hoping to make a small break. The window was stronger than he'd anticipated, so he had to hit it hard.

The glass shattered, making a distinct crashing sound. He froze, waiting to see if the cop would come running over to investigate.

A few minutes later, Griff worked on getting the shards of glass out of the way so he could get inside. The opening was smaller than he'd realized, and he was afraid he wouldn't be able to squeeze through.

Jenna would have fit through the window without a problem, but no matter how he tried to angle himself, his shoulders kept getting stuck.

After three attempts, he gave up. He'd have no choice but to pick up Jenna at the motel. They'd have to leave Claire alone for a few hours, but they'd be back before the teen realized they were gone.

Once he was back in the brown Dodge, he called Jenna. "I need your help," he said in lieu of a greeting.

"What happened?" she demanded. "I've been worried sick."

She wouldn't be happy to know that he'd intended to get inside his house without her. "I'm sorry. I want to sneak into my place, but there's a cop outside watching the door and I can't fit through the basement window."

There was a prolonged silence before she said, "Okay, what are we looking for?"

"I'll be there to pick you up in ten minutes and will explain on the way. Is Claire sleeping?"

"Yes, but I'll leave her a note in case she wakes up."

He was hesitant to leave Claire in the motel alone, but all they needed was a couple of hours. They hadn't been followed, so she should be safe enough.

Waiting in the car wasn't an option since Claire could be discovered by a cop cruising the neighborhood.

When he pulled around The Quilted Bee Motel, Griff saw Jenna waiting for him outside. She quickly slid into the passenger seat and fastened her seat belt.

"You were going to do this by yourself, huh?" she asked when he headed back out to the highway.

He sighed. "Only because I was already at the hospital, not because I was trying to hide anything from you."

She crossed her arms over her chest. "I still don't understand why you would have anything at your house that would help us with the case."

"I knew I'd heard the name Porchanski before and remembered that Helen was working on the child-custody case of a girl named Andrea Porchanski," he told her. "Maybe it doesn't mean anything, but I can't help wondering if the cases are linked somehow."

Jenna frowned. "A child-custody case is a long way from re-adoptions."

"Maybe, but I have to know one way or the other."

"I'm surprised your wife's files didn't get returned to the law firm."

"To be honest, her files weren't supposed to be removed from the office," he admitted. "Darnell was a stickler on that point, but when we fought about how little time we spent together, Helen secretly made copies of her files so she could work on them at home." He hesitated, then added, "After her death, I packed everything in boxes and stored them in the attic."

Jenna let out a low whistle. "So it's possible there is something in there that could help us."

"Yeah." He didn't say anything more until they were a few blocks from his house. "We'll walk from here."

"No problem."

He took Jenna's hand in his as they made their way to his backyard. Once again, he paused by the small evergreen tree to make sure nothing had changed in the time he was gone.

"Ready?" Jenna asked, obviously eager to get started.

"Sure." He pushed aside the sense of foreboding and led the way over to the broken basement window. "Be careful," he warned.

Jenna glanced up at him. "I can't believe you thought you'd fit through this," she chided softly.

"Yeah, well, I was obviously wrong about that. Now listen, this window is right above a large sink that's connected to my washer and dryer. Once you get inside, head up to the first floor and open the back door for me."

"Okay." Jenna stuck her head and arms through the window opening. He braced her legs until she had a hold on the sink below.

With athletic grace, Jenna wiggled inside, disappearing from view.

Griff moved away from the window to wait between the kitchen window and the back door. After what seemed like an endless period of time, Jenna opened the kitchen window so that he could crawl inside.

"What took you so long?" he asked as he closed the window.

"I didn't want to use a light, so I had to feel my way through the basement. Made a couple of wrong moves."

He took a deep breath and told himself to relax. "Follow me," he instructed.

Jenna stayed close behind him as he stealthily moved through his house, climbing the stairs that led to the second floor. He couldn't help remembering the last time they'd been here, fighting for their lives.

The entrance to the attic was through an opening in the ceiling just outside the master bedroom. He reached up and pulled the string that would lower the hidden fold-up stepladder.

Griff ascended first, visualizing the attic's layout. He hadn't been up here in the two years since Helen's death. Upon reaching the top, he moved to the side to give Jenna room to join him.

"We need some light," Jenna said in a soft voice. "Is there a window up here that we need to worry about?"

"No window, but there is a vent. It's on the back side of the house, so we should be okay." He pulled out his phone and turned on the flashlight application. "The boxes are over there," he said, indicating the stack against the south wall.

He pulled the top box down and opened the flaps. "You start with this one. I'll do the next."

"And we're only looking for the Andrea Porchanski case?" Jenna asked. "Or anything related to adoptions?"

He paused, wishing he could read her expression in the dim light. "Anything related to adoptions, I guess," he acknowledged.

"Right." Jenna began shifting through the files, leaving him to focus his attention on the next box.

Minutes ticked by slowly as he opened one file

at a time, skimming the contents for anything of interest. Griff was beginning to think he'd misunderstood the name Helen had mentioned, when he found the Porchanski file.

His chest tightened as he pulled out the folder and opened it up. Inside he found the custody paperwork related to one minor child, Andrea Porchanski.

From what he could see, there wasn't anything suspicious about the custody dispute. Andrea was thirteen and her mother didn't want to split custody fifty-fifty with her father, citing disruptive behavior as the reason Andrea needed the stability of a single home.

But then he stumbled upon the connection he'd dreaded.

Andrea had an older sister, Theresa, who was fifteen. Apparently Theresa had decided to live with her father full-time, rather than staying with her mother.

He sat back on his heels, his mind whirling with possibilities. Was Darnell targeting the kids of his clients? If that was the case, then Helen hadn't been involved in anything illegal.

A wave of relief hit hard, making him dizzy. He dropped his chin to his chest and tried to calm his racing heart.

"Griff?" Jenna's voice penetrated the haze clouding his mind. "I think you need to see this."

His knee-jerk reaction was to shout *no*, but

instead he lifted his head to meet Jenna's concerned gaze. She held out the file, and he found himself loath to take it.

"It's the adoption of a teenager roughly the same age as Claire," Jenna continued, as if his world wasn't crumbling around him. "And the adoptive parents are Steven and Dorie Tranberg. Same initials as Stuart and Debra Trent."

He took the file and opened it, staring down at the photograph of a pretty teenage girl with long dark hair and wide brown eyes.

His heart sank to the pit of his stomach as he realized his worst nightmare had come true.

His wife had participated in Darnell's re-adoption scheme.

# THIRTEEN

The stark expression of horror on Griff's face made Jenna want to kick herself for tossing the news about what she'd found at him so bluntly. Not that there was a gentle way to let him know about the re-adoption she'd uncovered, but she wished she'd considered taking the folder without mentioning the details to him.

"I'm sorry, Griff," she whispered helplessly. "I know this wasn't what you wanted to find."

He shook his head, his gaze downcast. "No, it wasn't," he said in a hoarse voice. "But there's no disputing the facts." He hesitated, then added, "Did you find any other adoption files?"

"Not yet." She wondered if he really wanted her to keep looking. Wasn't what they had found incriminating enough? "Maybe we should focus on the Porchanski case instead."

"I already have it." Griff lifted a green file folder with a grimace. "Andrea has an older sister,

Theresa. She was fifteen at the time of the custody dispute, so she's roughly Claire's age now."

Jenna's mind raced with that news. "What happened?"

"At the time of this custody battle, Theresa had decided to live with her father, and the judge upheld her decision."

"But that doesn't make sense," she said with a frown. "Her father wouldn't give her up for adoption. If things got rough, he'd be more likely to send her back to live with her mother."

He shrugged. "Unless she ran away or something happened to her father. We'll have to investigate further, but I can't help wondering if Darnell was using his clients as a way to target specific girls."

Jenna shivered, hating to admit that Griff might be right. At this point, she wouldn't put anything past Darnell Franklin and honestly couldn't wait to toss him in jail where he belonged.

It occurred to her that she hadn't told Griff about the link between Leo and Franklin. And he hadn't mentioned if Leo had provided any information they could use to find Stuart Trent, or Steven Tranberg, or whoever he was.

They'd sort through those details later. "I think we have enough information to work with," she said, focusing on the issue at hand. By her estimation they'd been in the attic for a good thirty minutes already. "Let's take both of these files back to the motel room. Claire's been there alone long enough."

Griff gave a curt nod and closed the boxes, restacking them the way they'd found them. She took both file folders and tucked them under her arm, wishing she could think of something to say that would make him feel better.

Even though they had the adoption folder as evidence, Jenna couldn't say for sure Helen was aware she was doing anything illegal. One might argue that, as a lawyer, Helen should have looked into something like that before going along with whatever her partners wanted.

Not all partners, but for sure Darnell.

Silence stretched between them as they maneuvered their way down to the second floor. She waited while Griff folded the ladder back up into the ceiling, then followed him as they crept down the stairs to the main level.

The Sheriff's Office vehicle was still parked out front, clearly visible through the living room window. Feeling like a fugitive, Jenna hugged the wall as they rounded the corner and crossed the kitchen to reach the door.

Griff opened it and then waved, indicating that she should head out first. She scanned the area, making sure no one had come around to investigate, before she lightly ran across the yard, stopping when she reached the small pine tree. Turning, she waited for Griff to join her.

He met up with her less than a minute later, and together they retraced their steps to the Dodge. It wasn't until they were inside and safely pulling away that Jenna breathed normally.

She didn't much care for operating on the wrong side of the law. Technically, they hadn't been stealing or trespassing, but sneaking past cops, knowing that they were wanted for questioning related to an officer-involved shooting, didn't sit well.

"Did Leo give you any information?" she asked, breaking the silence.

Griff nodded. "Claims the four-family apartment building is on Clayborn Street, a few miles north of the Wisconsin/Illinois border. I'm hoping Claire will recognize it when she sees it."

"That's great," Jenna said, glad to know they may be able to pinpoint where the girls had been held. "I'm worried that Darnell will find a way to get to Leo."

"Why would he?"

She took a moment to fill him in on the connection between Franklin and Affron.

"I wish I had known that when I talked to him," Griff admitted. "He didn't give me Darnell Franklin's name when I pressed him for information."

Jenna shrugged. "I guess it could be a coincidence, but I doubt it."

"We have Franklin connected to the man who broke into my place to grab Claire. We know Franklin also did the paperwork for Claire's adoption. Once we get the DNA results from the wound on your hand, we should be able to pinpoint the name of the guy who tried to attack you."

Hard to believe that they'd taken the DNA sample less than three days ago. It seemed much longer. "Dr. Gabby said getting the DNA results could take up to a month. We don't have that kind of time."

"I know."

"If only we could find Stuart Trent," Jenna muttered. "He's a big piece of the puzzle."

Griff was silent for a moment as he pulled into the parking lot of their motel. He drove around to the back and parked near their rooms. "I was thinking that once we locate the four-family apartment building, we should probably make a call to the FBI."

Jenna swallowed hard, wanting to protest but knowing he was right. They'd already connected several threads together, more than enough to hand the investigation over to the Feds. For all they knew, the FBI might have some insight into the human-trafficking ring.

"Agreed," she finally said. "You need to call the deputy chief, as well."

"That's settled, then," Griff said, pushing open

the driver's-side door. She climbed out of the car, as well, still carrying the files. Griff unlocked the door to his room, leading the way inside.

The connecting door between their rooms was open, the way she'd left it, but that didn't stop Jenna from checking to make sure Claire was still asleep.

The bed was empty.

Her heart leaped into her throat until she realized the bathroom door was closed. Drawing her weapon, she silently crossed over to listen by the door.

Nothing but silence.

Jenna tightened her grip on the gun, then reached out to turn the door handle. It wasn't locked, so she pushed the door open.

Claire was curled up in a ball inside the bathtub with a pillow, sound asleep. Jenna momentarily closed her eyes, sending up a silent prayer of thanks, before holstering her gun.

She leaned over the rim of the tub to put a gentle hand on her sister's shoulder. "Claire? Are you all right?"

The teen woke with a start, staring up at Jenna with wide, frightened eyes. Then she scrambled upright and launched herself at Jenna.

"You left me here alone," she said in an accusatory tone. "I was so scared."

"I'm sorry," Jenna murmured, holding Claire close. "Did something happen?"

Claire shook her head.

"You were sleeping," Jenna added. "I figured we'd be back before you woke up."

Claire hugged her as if she'd never let go. "Don't do that again," she begged.

"I won't," Jenna promised. She sensed Griff coming up behind her and glanced over her shoulder to meet his guilt-ridden gaze. "I should have known leaving a note wouldn't reassure you that we were fine."

"I was afraid you would get caught and that I'd be alone again." Claire finally released her grip on Jenna, drawing in a deep breath and wiping the dampness from her cheeks. "But maybe I overreacted."

"No, you have every right to be scared after everything you've been through," Jenna assured her.

"Get some sleep," Griff suggested, pinning Jenna with a look that warned her not to discuss anything they'd found. "We'll talk in the morning."

"It's already morning," Claire grumbled. But she headed into the bedroom and crawled beneath the covers.

Griff walked back to the opening between their rooms. Jenna glanced at the files she'd dropped on her table, but didn't move to take them.

Maybe he was right to hold off on doing anything more until they got some sleep. It was already two in the morning and they'd been up for nineteen hours straight.

"Good night, Jenna," Griff said from the doorway.

"Good night," she responded, watching as he partially closed the door between their rooms to give them a little privacy.

She stretched out on the bed fully dressed, and despite the exhaustion weighing her down, she stared blindly up at the ceiling.

Turning themselves in to their boss once Claire was able to pinpoint the location of the four-family apartment building was the right thing to do.

Yet she found herself regretting the fact that they would soon return to their professional relationship, losing the close partnership she'd come to cherish. Griff was an amazing man and she admired him more than ever.

She lightly touched her mouth, remembering his kiss.

Wishing she could repeat the experience once more, before their time together came to an end.

Griff had no clue why he bothered trying to sleep. Images of Helen handling the same type of adoption as Darnell Franklin remained imprinted in his mind until he couldn't stand it a second longer.

Splashing cold water on his face helped a little. When he lifted the screen of his laptop, he found the case search Jenna had done on Leo Affron.

Seeing Darnell's name in black and white as Affron's attorney only made him angrier. The guy had held back that tidbit of information.

What else had he held back?

Griff wanted to return to the hospital to confront the man with the truth. Obviously that wasn't possible at the moment, but he could only hope that, once he and Jenna turned themselves in, Deputy Chief Markham would allow him to continue working on the case.

He dropped his head into his hands, knowing he should grab the files Jenna had brought back with them and begin reviewing the data. But he couldn't make himself move, unable to face what he might find.

It was possible Helen hadn't quite understood what she was getting involved with, but he wasn't sure that he could accept the excuse of ignorance. The plain truth was that she should have known. She should have investigated what was at stake before getting mixed up in Franklin's scheme.

Apparently the lure of making money was too much to resist.

"Griff?" Jenna's voice startled him and he jerked upright. "Can't sleep, either, huh?"

"No," he agreed with a sigh. "I can't seem to shut down my brain long enough to fall asleep."

"Yeah, same here." He realized she had the file folders in her hands. "Listen, I was thinking that you should let me review these first. I could be wrong about the adoption. I only briefly glanced at the documents."

She wasn't wrong, and they both knew it. Jenna was trying to help him, obviously sensing his despair. "I'll be fine," he insisted.

Jenna pulled out a chair and sat down across from him. "It's not exactly fair to Helen that we're so ready to believe the worst about her. She's not here to defend herself."

"It's not just this issue with Helen," he murmured. "I've dedicated my entire life to upholding the law. Do you have any idea how awful it is to know that the people you loved didn't have the same respect for what's right or wrong?"

Her brow puckered in a puzzled frown. "I know a little about that now that I've found Claire. Have you looked at her rap sheet?"

Jenna's dry tone made him want to smile—no easy feat, considering what they'd discovered. "My parents died in a car crash when I was eight years old," he said. He'd never told anyone about his parents' criminal past, not even Helen.

"I'm sorry. That must have been terrible for you."

"It could have been worse. I was sent to live

with my grandparents. My grandmother taught me to open doors for women."

This time, Jenna grinned. "I shouldn't have been upset about that," she acknowledged. "I was being ridiculous."

"Yes, you were," he agreed. "But that wasn't the point of the story. I didn't learn until my early teens that my parents were actually swindlers. They convinced innocent people to invest money in their company, but they never paid out any profits. Instead, they kept all the money for themselves, spending it on boats, fancy cars and the huge mansion we lived in."

"How do you know that for sure?" she asked.

"I found a newspaper article that described how one of the men who'd lost everything rammed their car with his, causing the crash that ultimately claimed their lives."

She sucked in a harsh breath and leaned over to put a hand on his forearm. "That's terrible," she whispered. "He didn't have a right to kill them just because he was upset."

Griff liked the feel of her hand on his arm. "He claimed he only meant to scare them, not hurt them."

Jenna rolled her eyes. "Ridiculous," she scoffed. "Why didn't he go to the authorities instead? Why take matters into his own hands?"

"He did, but apparently no one could help him since he willingly gave them his money. They claimed the investments were legit, but the stock went bad. It was only later that he found out there was a full FBI white-collar crime investigation being conducted about their so-called investment scheme."

Jenna's penetrating gaze didn't miss much. "So that's the reason you went into law enforcement and why you've been such a stickler for following the rules."

"Until I rushed to your rescue," he added lightly. "Since then, following rules hasn't been my top priority."

Her gaze turned thoughtful. "I'm happy to take the blame for the way things unfolded," she said. "Ballistics will prove that my .38 was the weapon used to shoot Affron."

He stared at her in surprise, humbled by her willingness to take the heat. "That's nice, but the first perp's blood was likely found on my kitchen floor. Besides, I'm your boss. It's clear that I made a conscious decision to go along with you."

She sat back in her chair and he missed the warmth of her hand when she removed it from his arm. "I appreciate you sharing that with me," she said. "I guess we both had obstacles to overcome in our youth."

"You never told me why you care so much about the shelter," he said.

She grimaced and shrugged, but he could see

the tension in her face. "Same old story. Abusive father takes his anger out on his wife and daughter. Things escalated to the point he tried to kill us, but we managed to fight him off long enough for help to arrive."

Griff clenched his fingers into fists, hating the thought of Jenna going through something so terrible. "I hope he went to jail."

"He did, but he was just released on parole." She flashed a crooked smile. "I've been meaning to check things out, make sure the cops in his jurisdiction are aware of the permanent no-contact order I have, but there hasn't been much time to worry about that."

"I'll go with you," Griff offered darkly. "Happy to make sure the cops deliver the message loud and clear."

"Thanks, but I can take care of myself," she protested mildly. "Don't worry. I doubt he can hurt me anymore. On the day of his release, I saw a picture of him. He looked old and feeble, far from the monster from my dreams."

Griff knew she was a strong, capable deputy, clearly able to take care of herself, but he still didn't want her to face the man alone. Was this how things would be once they turned themselves in? He hated the thought of losing the camaraderie they shared.

He'd got used to having her as a partner and would miss her once this was over.

When she reached for the file folder, he stopped her by encircling her wrist with his fingers. "Let's let it go for now," he suggested. "We really do need to try to get some sleep."

"Are you sure?" she asked with a frown. "The sooner we get our facts in order, the sooner we can turn ourselves in."

For a long moment, he felt as if he could lose himself in her clear blue gaze. He searched for the words to explain how he felt. "Talking to you about my past, and hearing your story, as well, has helped to put everything in perspective," he said finally. "It makes me realize that neither one of us deserve to be saddled with the sins of our parents. We've chosen to uphold the law, not break it or skirt around the edges. We can be confident in the strength of our reputations."

"You're right," Jenna murmured. "For years I resented my father, but looking back, I can see that everything happened for a reason. Living in the shelter, learning about God and faith, has helped me become the woman I am today."

"My grandmother raised me to believe in God," he admitted. "I let my faith go to the wayside when my relationship with Helen began to fall apart."

She leaned forward, earnestly taking both of his hands in hers. "That's too bad," she said in a low husky voice. "Because that was the time you needed God the most."

He nodded, knowing she was right. "Thanks, Jenna," he said, before he captured her mouth in a heartfelt kiss.

# FOURTEEN

If asked, she would have denied that she'd made the decision to talk to Griff in the hopes she'd be given the chance to kiss him again.

But she couldn't deny being thrilled with the end result.

Unfortunately, Griff ended the kiss too soon. She reluctantly let his hands go and forced herself to take a deep breath as she sat back in her seat, hoping to calm her erratic pulse.

"Thanks, Jenna," Griff said in a gruff voice. "I appreciate your support, especially in helping me find my way back to my faith."

Knowing that he'd kissed her out of gratitude, and nothing more, sent a shaft of disappointment searing through her heart. But she tried not to let her feelings show on her face. "We've made a pretty good team," she agreed, rising to her feet, praying her knees wouldn't buckle. "And I'm sure you would have found your way back to God eventually, even without me."

"I'm not so sure about that," he said, his intense gaze boring into hers.

A sense of self-preservation prevented her from throwing herself back into his arms. "Good night, Griff."

"Good night," he murmured.

She could feel the lingering effects of his gaze as she made her way back through the connecting doorway. Sinking down onto the edge of the bed, she dropped her face into her hands and tried not to think about what could never be.

No reason to obsess over their brief kiss. Okay, maybe she was beginning to care about Griff on a personal level. That was her problem, not his.

She couldn't expect anything from him.

Their relationship would return to its previous professionalism once they'd turned this case over to the Feds. Being on the run, stuck in close proximity like this, wasn't normal.

In fact, it was no wonder that people fell into the trap of thinking that an emotional connection that had been developed during a crisis was enough of a base upon which to build a relationship. Too bad those same people didn't think about what would happen when the danger was gone. When the day-to-day reality of life would make them realize those emotions were only a temporary, heat-of-the-moment kind of thing. Not something that was mature enough to last forever.

Jenna knew she couldn't risk reading anything

serious into Griff's kiss. Not just for her own sake, but for Claire's. Her sister would need a dependable, stable environment in order to get back on track. To go to school, graduate, then attend college.

Getting involved with a man, even someone as handsome, strong and protective as Griff, would only complicate the issue. Something neither of them needed. Supervising a teenager wouldn't be a picnic.

Jenna crawled beneath the covers without fully undressing, thinking she'd just rest for a few minutes.

But the next time she opened her eyes, the early dawn light was seeping around the heavy curtain covering the window. Jenna frowned and swung herself upright, sensing she was alone even before she whipped around to stare at the empty bed beside hers.

Claire!

She bolted out of bed and quickly searched the bathroom, verifying it was empty before she barreled through the connecting door, her gaze raking over the interior of Griff's room. He'd been asleep, as well—dressed, fortunately—and he jerked upright when she came rushing in. "What's wrong?" he asked, reaching for his gun.

"Claire's gone." Stark terror gripped her about the throat, threatening to cut off her airway. "I take it you didn't hear anything unusual?"

"No." Griff frowned and brushed past her into the room she'd shared with her sister. He stood in the middle of the room and made a slow circle, seeming to absorb the environment. "There isn't any sign of a struggle."

Jenna raked a hand through her hair in frustration. "I'm sure I would have heard if someone had knocked or come inside," she said, although her tone lacked conviction.

Would she really? Or had her bone-deep exhaustion and cumulative lack of sleep finally caught up to her?

"Let's think logically," Griff said in a calm tone. "If we didn't hear anything unusual, then there's nothing to be worried about. She probably went over to the lobby for breakfast."

"Yeah. Okay, sure. Let's check." Jenna pulled on her shoulder holster, scooped up her .38 and quickly headed for the door. Outside, the cool March wind was like a shocking slap to the face, and when she exhaled she could see her breath. "When did the temperature drop?" she asked with a shiver.

"I don't know. We haven't been paying attention to the news," Griff said as he kept pace alongside her. They followed the sidewalk around the corner of the building to the front lobby.

By the time they reached the door, Jenna had convinced herself that they'd panicked over nothing. Claire wasn't a little kid. She'd probably got hungry and gone to breakfast, giving them time to catch up on their sleep.

Griff reached over Jenna's shoulder to open the door for her, and she walked inside, grateful for the cloak of warmth that enveloped her.

But then she stopped short, sweeping her gaze over the tiny interior of the lobby.

Claire wasn't anywhere in sight.

Jenna felt the room spinning around her, and she had to reach out and grasp Griff's arm to keep from crumpling to her knees. "I don't understand. Where is she?" she asked in a hoarse whisper.

"We'll find her," Griff said in a firm tone. "She's on foot. She can't have gone far."

Was she on foot? Jenna cast her mind back, trying to remember if she'd seen the brown Dodge.

"I have the keys," Griff said as if her thoughts were clearly written on her face. He pulled them out and dangled them in front of her.

"That's good," she murmured. Although, for some reason, knowing Claire hadn't taken the vehicle wasn't at all reassuring. Had she called someone to come and pick her up? And if so, why? "I'm going to try her phone." She dialed the number of the disposable phone they'd given to Claire, but she didn't pick up. Jenna swallowed hard and left a message. "Claire? Where are you?

Please call me back. I'm sorry if you're upset with me. Let's talk, okay? Call me."

She slid the phone into the back pocket of her jeans. "Hopefully she'll call us back." Then a thought occurred to her. "Wait a minute. Let's check the computer."

"Social media," Griff agreed, taking her hand as they jogged back to their rooms. "Maybe she's kept in touch with her old friends."

Jenna wasn't sure what to think. Claire had seemed contrite about getting into trouble while living with the Bronsons, had voiced her intent to turn her life around.

Maybe Claire was lashing out at Jenna for leaving her alone last night. Remembering the way she'd found Claire hiding in the bathroom, sleeping in the tub, made Jenna feel guilty all over again.

"We shouldn't have left her alone last night," she said as Griff turned on the computer. "She probably doesn't trust me anymore."

"That was a mistake on our part," Griff agreed. "But it doesn't make sense that her response would be to take off on her own without so much as a note telling us where she went."

Jenna nodded, but couldn't shake the feeling of dread that intensified with every minute that passed.

Griff went to the browser history and found a social-media page Claire must have accessed.

Jenna leaned closer, trying to get a clear look at the boy's face on the page. He had a lip ring and jet-black hair that hung over his eyes. "Python?" she asked in disbelief. "Claire was hanging out with a boy who calls himself Python?"

Griff didn't say anything, but clicked along the side of the page, revealing the messages that were sent. "She asked him to pick her up this morning," he said with a grimace.

"No, that can't be right." Jenna didn't want to believe Claire had just abandoned her without saying goodbye. But when Griff expanded the messages on the screen, the truth stared her in the face. "Why would she do this?" she asked, glancing up at Griff helplessly.

"I don't know," he said, blowing out his breath in a heavy sigh. "But we'll find her."

She wanted to believe Griff was right, but her stomach tightened with fear and worry.

Was it possible she'd lose her sister as quickly and unexpectedly as she'd found her?

Griff couldn't believe Claire had run off without saying a word. Especially when she'd seemed set on helping them find the place where the missing girls were held.

Without Claire, they didn't have a chance of pinpointing the apartment building on Clayborn Street.

"We need to find her," Griff said, breaking the silence.

"The message she sent to Python asks him to pick her up at the park-and-ride less than a mile away," Jenna said, her tone edged with despair. "But this was sent well over an hour ago. They're long gone by now."

"Are you sure?" Griff propelled her toward the door. "Let's go see if Python really moves as fast as his namesake."

They ran out to the brown Dodge, and Griff gunned the engine, tires squealing as he drove toward the park-and-ride. It was the same place where they'd met with Shane to swap vehicles.

It was also far away from where the Bronsons lived.

When they got there, Griff turned into the lot and slowed to a crawl. Jenna had her face pressed up against the passenger-side window, clearly searching for any sign that Claire was still in the vicinity.

There were no pedestrians, probably because of the change in the weather. Griff hated to think of Claire being outside in the cold, wearing nothing more than a sweatshirt.

He turned his attention to the cars parked in the area, wondering if it was possible that Python had come to pick Claire up, but that they hadn't left yet. When he caught sight of a rusty white Camaro with foggy windows, he drove over and parked behind it, blocking it in so they couldn't leave.

"Do you think they're inside?" Jenna asked, fear giving way to hope.

"We'll soon find out," he said in a grim tone. He slid out from behind the wheel and then pounded on the driver's-side window. "Open up! Police!"

The vehicle rocked a bit before the window opened to reveal a red-haired boy with freckles staring up at him sheepishly. "What's wrong? We're just—talking. You can't arrest us for that." He looked nervous as he held his hands up, as if he'd done this before.

This guy wasn't Python. Griff bent down to get a good look at the girl, a brunette who was sitting with her arms crossed over her chest. Not Claire. "Get out of here," Griff said in a stern tone. "Go home."

The kid shot him an exasperated look. "You mean go to school, right?"

Griff had lost track of the fact that it was now Monday morning. "Yeah, that's right, school," he amended. He stepped back and caught Jenna's gaze, giving her a shake of his head. "Wrong car."

He had to move the Dodge in order for the teens to back out and head off to school. He continued driving around the parking lot, catching a glimpse of another car, this one a black truck badly in need of a new muffler.

He was sure that was Claire in the passenger seat. He cranked the steering wheel to the right, making a sharp turn in order to follow the truck.

Jenna pulled out her phone and tried calling Claire again. "Pick up. Please pick up!" she muttered.

Griff kept his attention focused on not losing the truck, especially when the driver sped up. Python must have realized they were hot on his tail since he started driving erratically, taking several turns in an effort to shake them off, making Griff wish they still had the squad car so they could go lights and sirens.

"Don't lose them," Jenna begged as she braced herself with a hand on the dashboard.

"I won't." From the corner of his eye, he noticed she was attempting to reach Claire through text messages.

He punched the gas when Python shot across two lanes of traffic to get onto the interstate. Thankfully the Dodge was able to keep up, but Griff knew that it wouldn't take long to attract attention from the patrol officers on duty.

Something he'd rather avoid, if possible.

Maybe Python knew that, too, since he slowed to a respectable pace, right at the speed limit.

"She responded," Jenna said excitedly. "She's telling him to take the next exit."

Griff gave a wary nod, knowing that Claire might be trying to pull a fast one. When the right-hand blinker flashed from the black truck, Griff put his on, as well, staying as close to the truck's back end as he dared.

He relaxed his grip when Python actually exited the interstate, turning right again at the end of the off-ramp. "Tell Claire to pull into the gas station ahead."

Jenna's fingers flew over the buttons, relaying the message. Sure enough, the truck entered the gas station and pulled over.

Griff parked alongside the truck, glancing over to look at Claire. He was relieved when she met his gaze and mouthed the words *I'm sorry.*

"Maybe you should go talk to her," Griff said, keeping the engine running just in case Python tried to slither away. "I don't trust the guy."

Jenna didn't waste a second but quickly sprang from the car and hurried over to where Claire waited with her window rolled down. Griff lowered his window, too, so he could hear the conversation.

"I'm sorry. Please come back with us," Jenna was saying. "I know you're upset, but running away isn't the answer. Let's talk."

"I'm not trying to run away," Claire said. "I think I found Shaunee, the girl who gave me the penknife."

"What?" Griff leaned his head out the window, inserting himself into the conversation. Jenna took a step back, so he could see Claire. "Where?"

"Dude, you gotta back off, man," Python drawled. "We're just takin' a ride."

"I don't understand. Why did you leave? Haven't we been helping you all along?" Jenna pressed, reaching out to touch Claire's shoulder. "If you found something about Shaunee, then we'll help you find her."

Claire ducked her head, obviously swamped with guilt. "I'm not even sure she'll be there, but she mentioned a place called Gulliver's Grub, so I thought we'd go check it out."

The place sounded like a dive, one Claire had no business going into alone or with a guy who was nicknamed after a snake. "We'll check it out with you," Griff said. "Come on, Claire. We need to stick together."

For a long moment Claire looked at him, then at Jenna. "All right. Sorry, Python. I'm going with my sister."

Claire moved to get out of the car, but Python lived up to his name, reaching out to grab her arm in a tight grip. "What about the money you promised?" he demanded. "I'm not leaving without it."

"Let go of her," Jenna said fiercely, yanking open the passenger door. "Don't make me arrest you for assault."

This time, Python didn't move fast enough. Jenna grabbed his hand and pushed on the joint between his thumb and first finger with enough force to make him let go. He snatched his hand back, then scowled.

Claire clambered out, casting an apologetic glance at Python. "I forgot to tell you my sister is a cop," she said.

Jenna stepped protectively in front of Claire. "You have two minutes to get lost," she said in a hard tone. "I don't want to see you hanging around Claire ever again, understand?"

The teen sulked and muttered a curse under his breath. Jenna urged Claire to get into the Dodge's backseat, waiting for Python to leave.

Griff was just about to get out of the car to offer his assistance, when the teen put the truck in Reverse and backed up. The muffler rattled loudly as Python shifted gears and headed onto the road.

Jenna strolled around the car and slid into the passenger seat. Before snapping her seat belt into place, she turned to face Claire. "Why did you leave like that? What did I do wrong?"

Griff watched Claire squirm as she struggled with a response. "I don't know," she said finally. "I guess I was still upset that you guys left me alone last night. You said we needed to stick together, but that's only when it's convenient for you."

"I left you a note," Jenna reminded her. "And you didn't bother to answer your phone. I was so afraid something horrible happened to you."

Claire ducked her head and picked at a spot on her sweatshirt. "I wasn't sure you'd miss me."

"We did miss you," Griff said firmly. "You're right. We messed up, but next time, talk to us rather than taking off."

"Do you really think we're like the Bronsons?" Jenna asked. "I know you took off a lot when you lived with them, but I thought things were different now. You're my sister, Claire. No matter what happens I'll always be there for you."

"I'm sorry," Claire said, her tone full of regret. "You're right. I shouldn't have messaged Python. He's pretty much a loser anyway, but he was the only guy I knew that had a car."

As much as Griff wanted to know all about Python, especially his real name, he turned the conversation back to the reason Claire left in the first place. "Did you really find Shaunee on social media?"

"I think so," Claire said, appearing grateful for the change of subject. "I scrolled through all the Shaunees in the Milwaukee/Chicago area and managed to stumble across her page. At least, I think it's her page. She doesn't post often, but yesterday she wrote something about Gulliver's Grub, a horrible place to call home. I think she was calling out for help."

"I'm surprised she's on social media," Jenna murmured.

"Maybe the girls get some latitude once he has them hooked on drugs," Griff said in a grim tone.

"Can we check it out?" Jenna asked.

Griff shrugged and nodded. "We'll go there first, but then we really need to search Clayborn Street."

"I have the address," Claire said, handing Jenna a slip of paper. "If we find Shaunee, then we won't need to go to Clayborn Street."

Griff backed out of the gas-station parking lot and drove back to the interstate, finally understanding the source of Claire's distress.

As much as she wanted to find the girls who'd suffered at Stuart Trent's hands, she was deathly afraid of going back to the place it all started.

He couldn't blame her, but somehow she needed to get beyond her fear, or they risked never holding those men accountable for what they'd done.

# FIFTEEN

Now that Claire was safe in their car, far away from the jerk she'd gone running to, Jenna wrestled with a myriad of emotions—a mixture of relief, frustration, anger and guilt, but predominately anger.

The way Claire had taken off hurt. A lot. How was it possible that Claire had done the same thing to Jenna as she had the Bronsons? What terrible transgression had Jenna done to deserve that? Was this all really because she'd left with Griff the night before? Or was Claire having second thoughts about living with her once they'd found a way out of this mess?

It seemed that running was Claire's go-to response when things didn't go the way she wanted them to.

For the first time since hearing Claire talk about the Bronsons, Jenna was forced to admit that maybe she'd misjudged the older couple. Maybe they hadn't been as awful as Claire had claimed.

She was beginning to believe Claire owned a big piece of the problem. That her sister preferred spending time with that loser over living a normal life, going to school and being involved in extracurricular activities.

The teen who'd driven the truck hadn't looked as if he was interested in anything remotely sporty or club-like.

The guy really was a snake.

"Python?" she blurted out in an exasperated tone, turning to look back at Claire. "Really? He calls himself Python?"

Claire rolled her eyes. "Pete got his nickname because he owns a python," she said. "Not because he looks like one."

Griff let out a strangled laugh that he tried to turn into a cough, but Jenna narrowed her eyes, not the least bit amused. Although she was forced to admit the kid did have an oddly shaped head, just like a snake. "Pete what?" she demanded.

"Baker." Claire tucked a strand of her long blond hair behind her ear. "Chill, Jenna. You're not my mother," she added in the bored tone used by teenagers across the globe.

"No, I'm not. But that doesn't mean there won't be rules at my house," Jenna said sternly. "Rules like you don't take off without telling me where you're going."

"Whatever," Claire mumbled, turning to stare out the window.

Jenna sighed, wondering what she'd got herself into. She'd invited her sister to stay with her without appreciating the challenges of living with a sixteen-year-old. Was this what she had to look forward to? Searching for Claire every time she became upset?

"I suppose you're going to give up on me, too," Claire said defiantly.

"No, I'm not," Jenna said firmly. Deep down, she knew that no matter how difficult things would be, she wouldn't turn her back on Claire. "But I wasn't joking about the rules. You're going to stop running at the first sign of trouble, and I'll help you get through school. We'll take it one day at a time, figuring things out together."

Claire didn't say anything, but Jenna thought she saw a hint of relief in her sister's blue eyes.

"Pete Baker, huh? What high school does he attend?" Griff asked.

There was a long silence. "Oakdale High," Claire finally said.

Jenna glanced at her watch, grimacing at the fact that it was already ten in the morning. "He's late," she said.

"Yeah, well, he doesn't always go to class," Claire admitted, plucking at her sweatshirt again. "School's boring."

Jenna reached out and placed a reassuring hand on her sister's knee. "You'll be able to catch up," she said, sensing Claire's hopelessness. "They have online programs now, which will help. And if that doesn't work, then we'll enroll in a program where you can obtain a GED."

"Why is graduating from high school so important to you?" Claire asked. "It's not like I'm smart enough to get into college. I'll just end up in some stupid routine job that I'll hate."

"That's not true. You can do anything you want to do," Jenna said. "Trust me. I missed a lot of school, especially before we ended up at the shelter. But I knew I wanted to be a police officer more than anything, so I worked hard to get caught up."

"Easy for you, but I don't have a clue what I want to do," Claire said.

"There's plenty of time. Don't start stressing over it now," Griff said. "We have other issues, like finding Shaunee."

Claire seemed to relax at that, so Jenna turned to face the front, glancing down at the address sitting on the console between them. "How much longer until we get to Gulliver's Grub?" she asked. Her stomach rumbled with hunger, yet the name of the place did not sound the least bit enticing.

The owner had picked a lousy marketing strategy.

"Another few miles," Griff said. "But the neighborhood seems to be going downhill."

He was right about that. The houses were

small, run-down and crowded together on streets that were littered with garbage. Despite the coolness in the air, they passed houses with an occasional broken window.

Could Gulliver's Grub be an apartment building, rather than a tavern? Jenna scanned the dwellings, searching for any identifying marks.

"This isn't Clayborn Street, is it?" Claire's voice was subdued, as if she were afraid someone would overhear.

"No, why?" Griff asked. "Does this area look familiar?"

Claire shrugged. "I don't know—maybe. When I was running away, I passed a lot of streets, but made sure I kept going in one direction so I wouldn't get lost or accidentally go in a circle ending up back there."

The image of Claire running for her life brought on another wave of guilt. So what if her sister had freaked out earlier this morning? The poor kid had been through a nightmare of an experience. Claire just needed to learn how to cope better, and surely having a stable home life would be a step in the right direction.

"I think that's it," Griff said in a grim tone as they approached a weather-beaten building sitting on the corner of Shamrock and Lilly Streets. Not a single light was on inside the building, and there weren't any cars in the postage-stamp-sized parking lot, either.

"They're not open yet," Jenna said with a sigh. "I guess we should have expected that."

"There's a sign on the door." Griff swung the Dodge into the parking lot. "Might list the hours."

"I'll check it out." Jenna ducked out of the car before Griff could argue, needing a bit of distance. The cold wind stole her breath, but she hunched her shoulders and hurried around the corner of the building to peer at the sign on the front door.

The hours of operation were from noon until two o'clock in the morning, Monday through Sunday. They were a good hour early, and the thought of sitting and waiting in the cold for the tavern to open didn't appeal.

Besides, it was clear Shaunee wasn't there now, and there was no guarantee that she'd be there the minute they opened, either. Jenna cupped her hands around her face and peered through the window. The interior of the place didn't look much better than the outside.

For a moment she thought she caught a glimpse of someone moving around toward the back. She stayed where she was, but if someone had been there, they were gone now.

Jenna stepped away from the building, then walked over to pull on the door. It was locked up tight. The back door? She hurried around to the other side of the building, only to discover that door was locked, too.

Must have been her imagination. She trudged back to where Griff and Claire were waiting. "Unfortunately, the place doesn't open until noon."

"Did you see something?" Griff asked, glancing up from his cell phone.

"I don't know. There could have been someone inside," she admitted. "It was just a brief flash, but even if there was, they obviously didn't want to talk to me."

"Both doors locked?" Griff asked.

She nodded. "Now what?"

Griff turned in his seat so that he was facing Jenna yet could still see Claire. "Are you sure this place doesn't look familiar?" he asked.

Claire frowned and gazed out the window. "I don't think so."

"Why?" Jenna asked, sensing there was a reason Griff was pushing the issue.

He lifted the phone, showing a map of the tavern's location. "This place happens to be two blocks away from Clayborn Street."

Claire gasped and Jenna's stomach twisted.

If they were that close to Clayborn Street, then it was entirely possible that Shaunee was also somewhere nearby.

Claire's quest to find Shaunee had actually helped steer them in the right direction. But as

Jenna looked over at her sister's deathly pale face, she could only hope and pray Claire had the strength to keep going.

They needed the location of the four-family apartment building that Stuart Trent had used as a staging area for the girls.

Once they had that information, they could turn everything over to the FBI and go home.

Griff could barely contain a surge of satisfaction that they were finally on the right track.

The way Claire had tracked down Shaunee was brilliant. They were so close to gathering the information they needed.

"Are you ready to cruise Clayborn Street?" he asked, trying to gauge Claire's mood. The teen looked scared, yet at the same time, resolved.

"Yeah," Claire said softly.

"Do you want me to sit in back with you?" Jenna offered, her expression full of concern.

Claire shook her head. "I'm all right. Let's go. I need to help Shaunee the same way she helped me."

Griff gave her a reassuring smile. "Good girl," he said with approval. "Just remember we're not going to do anything that will put you in danger. All we need is the address. From there, we'll call my boss and hand everything over to him."

"Then we'll go home?" Claire asked wistfully.

He hesitated, unwilling to lie. "Eventually, but

not right away. Not until these guys are arrested and we're certain you're out of danger."

Claire didn't look happy about that, but she nodded. "Okay, let's do it."

He exchanged a questioning look with Jenna, who nodded. "I'm on board, too."

After a brief moment of hesitation, he headed back out onto Shamrock. According to the online map, Shamrock would take him across Clayborn.

The intersection was just two blocks away, and he inwardly debated whether to go north or south. Since Chicago was located to the south, he decided to head north, figuring that Claire would have had to come from that direction in order to pass by Gulliver's Grub.

There was some traffic on the side streets, enough that he couldn't drive as slowly as he would have liked. Claire was quiet as she gazed out the window, no doubt remembering the night she'd been forced to fight for her life against a man twice her size in order to escape.

But he was afraid it wouldn't be as simple as he'd hoped for her to recognize the place in the light of day. She'd escaped at night, when the darkness and the shadows made everything look different.

After four blocks, he made a U-turn to head in the opposite direction. Maybe he'd been wrong to go this far north. Claire might not have passed by Gulliver's Grub.

"I just don't know," Claire wailed as they ended up right back where they'd started. "None of these places look at all familiar."

"It's okay," Jenna said. "We'll try again."

Griff met Claire's gaze in the rearview mirror. "Nighttime makes things look different. See if you can try imagining the buildings at night instead."

Claire's eyes welled up with tears. "You don't understand! I was scared and cold, running as fast as I possibly could go. I didn't pay that much attention to the buildings. My goal was to never come back here, ever."

"I do understand and I'm not blaming you at all. I doubt I would have paid attention, either. If you can't find the place, then that's all right. We'll just go in with what we have."

"I want to find it." Claire swiped away the tears in a gesture of frustration. "I want to help find Shaunee and the others."

"Okay, let's try looking at this from a different angle," Jenna said. "Why don't you tell us what you do remember? Was there anything that stuck out in your mind? The shape of a tree, or a particular building that you noticed looked different from the others?"

Griff was driving north again, slower this time since there wasn't anyone behind them. "That building there has a mailbox shaped like a barn," he said. "And that tree has really low branches."

"That fence," Claire said, slapping her hand on the window. "I'm pretty sure I climbed over that white fence."

"Over it?" Jenna exclaimed in surprise. "Griff, turn right at the next intersection. Maybe Leo got the name of the street wrong."

Griff wasn't so sure about that, but he did as Jenna directed, going around the block to the street that ran parallel to Clayborn.

"No, this isn't right," Claire muttered.

Griff was beginning to think this might be an impossible task. "I don't think Leo was lying to me," he said in an undertone to Jenna. "It's more likely that Claire zigzagged around in her haste to get away from the apartment building."

He completed the circle until he was back on Clayborn. This time, he went farther north, thinking that Claire may have run a lot longer than she realized.

"Wait," Claire said in a rush, reaching up to squeeze his shoulder. "Look!"

At what? The black van? Griff caught a glimpse of the vehicle and closed the distance between them. "Get the license-plate number," he told Jenna, who was already writing it on a slip of paper.

"I remember being taken to the apartment building in a black van just like that one," Claire whispered, as if fearing the occupants of the van might hear her. "I think it's the same one."

Griff sent a skeptical glance toward Jenna. "There are a lot of minivans in the city," he hedged. "This one could belong to anyone. What makes you think it's the same?"

"Try getting closer," Claire urged. "Can you tell if the passenger-side mirror is cracked? I remember staring at it, thinking my life was just as broken."

"Should I call the plate number in? See if we can get a name?" Jenna asked, holding her phone ready.

Griff eased up as close as he dared, his heart leaping into his throat when he saw the crack running diagonally through the passenger-side mirror. "Yeah, call it in," he said.

"It's slowing down," Claire said, ducking her head to avoid being seen. "That must be the apartment building."

Sure enough, the vehicle turned at the corner and then turned again, into a small parking lot behind two four-family apartment buildings. Griff passed the entrance to the parking lot, turned around and pulled to the side of the road where they could keep the van in sight.

"Call Shane, tell him where we are," Griff said. "We'll wait here until the team shows up."

"No, we can't just sit here doing nothing if there are girls inside," Claire protested, popping her head back up to glare at him. "We have to do something before they get a chance to drug them."

"Calm down," he said, but she interrupted him.

"I can't calm down! We have to get to those girls right away!"

Griff heard Jenna making the call to Shane, giving their coordinates. He kept his gaze pinned on the black van, hoping Claire was wrong about the possibility of young girls being trapped inside.

What were the chances of Stuart Trent and his cohorts bringing girls here this early in the morning? Claire mentioned running away at night, not in the middle of the day.

"Do you want to call your boss? And the FBI?" Jenna asked when she'd finished with Shane. "We need all the resources we can get."

"Yeah." He took the phone and punched in the number. This was it. Time to face Herb Markham's wrath.

While waiting for the deputy chief to pick up, Griff tried not to think about when he'd be able to see Jenna again outside of work. Not that she'd given him any indication that she wanted to see him on a personal level.

Well, other than that electrifying kiss.

"Markham," the deputy chief of operations barked in his ear.

"Sir? This is Lieutenant Vaughn, and we have a situation."

"Where have you been?" Markham roared

with such force Griff had to pull the phone away from his ear.

He winced. "Listen, I need you to contact the FBI. We're sitting outside one of the staging areas for a human-trafficking ring."

"What? Have you lost your mind? Is Deputy Reed with you? I want both of you to report to my office immediately."

Griff was forced to wonder if this was how ridiculous he'd sounded when he'd told his deputies to follow the rules. "Sir, contact the FBI. Give them this address and license-plate number." He rattled off the information, hoping the deputy chief was writing everything down. "We need backup, right away, understand?"

"Griff, look!" He nearly dropped the phone when Claire grabbed his arm and shook him. "There are two men taking two girls out of the van!"

He couldn't believe what he was seeing. Without hesitation, he disconnected the call with his boss and slipped the phone back into his pocket.

"Do something," Claire begged.

He glanced at Jenna. "How long before the rest of the team gets here?" he asked, knowing that no matter what time frame she told him, it would be too long.

"At least twenty minutes."

The sheer anguish radiating from Claire was impossible to ignore. There was no time to waste.

They needed to take immediate action to prevent any of these girls from being drugged.

Or worse.

# SIXTEEN

Jenna knew there was no way they could sit here and wait for backup. "Claire, do you know how to drive?"

Her sister nodded. "Yes, but I'm not leaving."

"Oh, yes, you are." Jenna's tone was firm. "I want you to call 911 to let them know that there are two deputies in need of assistance. They won't like it, since we're well outside our jurisdiction, but too bad."

"They need to come quietly, no lights or sirens," Griff added. "After you make the call, you need to drive to the nearest police station. Tell them your story, starting at the beginning."

It was clear Claire didn't want to leave, but Jenna was not taking no for an answer. "We're not going in until you're gone," she warned.

"Okay, I'll do it. Call 911 then drive to the nearest police station."

"Good." Jenna glanced at Griff. "Ready?"

He gave a curt nod. "See the evergreen across

from the parking lot? We'll meet there and plan our next move."

"Sounds good." Jenna pushed open her door and slid out. Griff did the same, but left the car engine running. Once Claire eased into the driver's seat, Jenna flashed her sister a thumbs-up before crouching down and following Griff as he headed toward the evergreen tree.

Jenna met Griff, then glanced back, frowning when she saw that Claire hadn't driven away yet. She waved impatiently, relaxing a bit when the Dodge eased away from the curb and headed down the street.

"So, what's the plan?" Jenna asked. "We've seen two men handling the girls, but there could be others inside."

"We'll need to split up," Griff decided. "You head around to the front, and I'll stay here in the back."

He was trying to protect her again, but she suspected that Griff would have made the same assignments even if she were one of the guys. Being close to Griff made her realize that he would always take the riskier approach himself, rather than exposing anyone else to danger. "The girls might feel safer if they see me instead of another man, especially since we're not in uniform."

He scowled, then let out a heavy sigh. "You

might be right, but I don't want to leave you back here alone," he grudgingly admitted.

"If we can eliminate whoever is out here, then the odds will be in our favor. Maybe the locals will show up by then." Realistically, it might be better to partner up with Griff rather than splitting up anyway.

At that moment, the back door of the apartment building opened and a tall, burly man stepped outside. Jenna reached out to grab Griff's arm. "Look, he's heading back to the van. Someone must still be inside. This is our chance."

"All right, let's go." Griff gave her hand a quick squeeze, then darted to the left while she went to the right.

The burly guy didn't notice them right away, his attention seemingly focused on whoever was still inside the van. Jenna bided her time, waiting for the moment he was close enough to the van that he wouldn't see them approach. There wasn't anywhere to hide between the evergreen tree and the parking lot.

She and Griff both moved at the same time, rushing forward to surround the vehicle. Griff had taken the front, leaving her with the back.

"No, please, don't! Leave me alone," the girl inside the van sobbed. She sounded young, and her cry for help hit Jenna hard, making her more determined than ever to get this guy.

"Shut up," the burly man said, reaching inside the van as if to grab her.

Jenna sent up a quick prayer, then sprang forward, catching the thug off guard. She grabbed his left arm and pulled it behind him, at the same time she firmly pressed the tip of her gun to the center of his back. "Police! Don't move, or I'll shoot."

The girl's eyes widened in shock, and she shrank away from the open doorway until she was plastered against the far side of the van. Jenna noticed the girl was not just tied up, but also tied to the door handle, preventing her from escaping.

"What?" The guy didn't listen, turning toward her and swinging with his other arm, his fingers curled into a thick fist. Jenna had a mental flashback of the guy who'd attacked her outside her home a few days ago.

Was this the same man? He didn't smell like cigar smoke, but that might not mean much.

Griff chose that moment to leap out from the other side of the van, grabbing the guy's arm before he could make contact with Jenna's face. Griff bent the man's arm behind him and thrust his gun into the guy's side. "You heard her— don't move. We've got you surrounded."

The thug opened his mouth as if to call for reinforcements, leaving Jenna little choice but to bring her knee up into his stomach hard enough to steal his breath.

When he grunted and bent over in shock, Griff shoved him to the ground, planting his knee in the center of the guy's back to pin him in place while Jenna quickly searched him for a weapon. "Don't say anything or we will shoot, understand?"

The guy nodded and she found the gun he'd stuffed in the waistband of his pants. She pulled it out and handed the weapon to Griff.

"Thanks. Now we need to tie him up," Griff said.

She glanced up at the girl, who was staring at them as if trying to figure out if they were friend or foe. The girl's freckles stood out against her pale face and Jenna recognized her as Theresa Porchanski. "Be quiet," she warned in a whisper. Then she turned to Griff. "Can you hold him without me?"

"Yeah." Griff shifted his weight so that both his knees were planted on the guy. He took the guy's left wrist from her grasp and pulled upward, making the man groan.

Jenna didn't waste any time getting into the van. "Hi, Theresa. I'm a police officer and I'm not going to hurt you, okay? I just need that rope from around your wrists."

The redhead scooched as close as she could, holding out her bound wrists. As Jenna removed the ties, she glanced around, making sure the rest of the van was empty.

"How many other girls are inside?" Jenna asked, freeing the girl. She took the rope and quickly crawled back outside, turning her attention to binding the wrists of the man they'd captured.

"I'm—not sure. Th-three others besides me were in the van," Theresa answered in a shaky voice. "Wh-who are you?"

Griff glanced up and flashed a reassuring smile. "We're both off-duty police officers. You're safe now, but we need to know how many men are still inside."

"I don't know," Theresa said helplessly. "They left me for last."

"How many men were in the van?" Jenna asked, trying another tactic. "Was this guy one of them? Or was he here at the apartment building already?" She nudged him with her foot.

"Yes. No, I'm not sure." Theresa's eyes filled with tears. "There were two men in the van with us. I can't tell if he was one of them or not."

"That's fine. We'll figure it out," Jenna assured her. "Listen, you need to get out and start running. Head south and flag down the first cop you see, understand?"

Theresa nodded and scrambled out of the van so quickly she tripped and fell to her knees. Jenna reached down and gave her a hand, wishing she could get into the details of how the girl ended up here. But there wasn't time.

"Go," Jenna urged, giving her a slight push, desperate for her to leave. "Find someplace safe."

Theresa nodded and ran, heading north instead of south, but Jenna figured there might be cops coming from that direction, too.

"Let's get him inside the van," Griff said. "Hurry—we've been out here too long already. One of the others will likely come out to investigate what's happening."

Jenna knew Griff was right. So far they'd taken out only one man, and there were others inside. At least two, but more likely three, one for each girl, by her estimation.

She grabbed the guy's left side at the same time Griff yanked on his right. They dragged him upright and shoved him through the open door of the van. Then she noticed other bindings on the floor, behind the bench seat.

"Let's tie his legs and gag him," Jenna said.

Griff nodded and they made quick work of securing their prisoner. Afterward, they climbed out of the van and shut the door, locking him inside.

Jenna exchanged a glance with Griff and with silent agreement they flanked the back door leading inside the fourplex. They could bust in, but knew that it was likely the men inside were armed.

Although if they waited out here for backup, the girls would be exposed to danger. She couldn't hear the telltale sounds of sirens, which was good since they didn't want to spook the perps.

Griff held up a hand with three fingers, indicating they'd move on his cue. When his index finger dropped, she opened the door, leaving him to ease inside first. Griff led with his gun, stepping softly as he hovered close to the right side of the short hallway with apartment doors located on each side. One of them was hanging ajar, as if someone had recently come through. Griff pushed the door open and then pressed himself against the right side of the wall.

Jenna followed, taking the left, straining to listen. The sound of girls crying was distracting, and she tried to shut out their sobs, focusing on pinpointing the male voices.

Were there two voices or three? And which way were they coming from?

She met Griff's gaze and pointed toward the opening that she felt sure led to the two bedrooms. From what Claire had described about the night she'd escaped, the men were likely holding the girls there.

Unfortunately, if there was a third man stationed in the kitchen or living room keeping watch on things, their plan was sunk.

"Ouch! Hey, she bit me," a male voice exclaimed. The shout was followed by a loud slap and more sobbing.

*No!* Jenna couldn't stand it another minute. She had to do something to save these girls. She gave Griff the go signal, ignoring him when he shook his head and darting up to the opening leading to the bedrooms.

The first one revealed a bald man roughly the same size as the guy they'd left outside, pinning a girl to the mattress of a twin-size bed. A wave of fury washed over her, to the point that she barely registered that there was a second girl tied to the bed on the other side of the room.

She hit the guy on the back of his bald head with the butt of her gun with as much force as she could muster.

The man let out a moan before he collapsed onto the bed. Jenna yanked him off the poor girl, who was still sobbing loudly.

"Shh," Jenna warned, glancing over her shoulder fearfully. How much time did they have before the others came running?

Griff had followed her into the room and was working hard to release the brunette from the bed. His jaw was tense when he tossed the bindings at Jenna, giving her the impression he was not happy with her decision.

She hated disappointing Griff, but couldn't regret taking the chance to save these girls. Using the rope to truss up Baldy, she marveled that they'd already taken two of the thugs out of the picture without firing a single shot. And from what she could tell, they'd got to the two girls before they'd been given any drugs, another thing to be thankful for.

Griff was moving toward the door, and she took a moment to hand Baldy's gun to the brunette. "Defend yourself and help free the other girl," she whispered, before following Griff.

But she'd barely taken two steps when Griff ducked and threw himself up against the wall. She dropped behind the closest bed, which didn't offer much protection.

"Hey, what's going on?" Another man came rushing into the bedroom. She lifted her head. When he locked gazes with Jenna, his eyes widened in recognition. She didn't need the stinky scent of stale cigar smoke to know he was the one who'd attacked her outside her home.

He fired his gun a split second before she could do the same.

Pain blazed in her shoulder, but she struggled to ignore it, staring at the guy who'd attacked her.

She lifted her gun hand, intending to return fire, but realized that her arm wasn't working properly. Blood ran in rivulets down her arm, and her .38 dropped to the floor, bouncing on the carpet.

Jenna swallowed hard, bracing herself to take another bullet.

* * *

Griff stared in horror at the blood running from the wound in Jenna's right shoulder. He instinctively fired his weapon in response, relieved when the guy collapsed without further incident.

But before he could cross over to offer aid to Jenna, another man came barreling through the door, gun blazing. Griff aimed and fired, praying there weren't any others. He heard a loud thud followed by dozens of footsteps stampeding into the building.

It took only a moment to register several officers covered from head to toe in SWAT gear.

His team had arrived, sooner than expected. Along with the local police.

"Check the other bedroom," he ordered. "And there's a man tied up in the van out back."

The officers did as they were told, leaving him to scramble over to Jenna, who sagged against the mattress, holding a hand over the wound in her shoulder.

"Hang on, Jenna," he urged, grabbing the sheets from the bed to use as bandages. "You're going to be fine, understand?"

Her blue eyes were wide as they locked onto his. "I can't feel my right arm," she whispered.

Griff swallowed hard, realizing that it was her gun hand. If the nerve had been severed, Jenna might not be able to remain on active duty.

"You're going to be just fine," he reiterated, hoping he wasn't wrong.

But Jenna wasn't buying it. She dropped her gaze from his and turned her head away in despair.

"The place is clear," someone shouted from the second bedroom. Griff continued holding pressure on Jenna's entry and exit wounds.

"We need an ambulance, stat!" he called.

Two figures appeared in the doorway, and he recognized Shane and Declan, both men looking grim when they saw Jenna's injury.

"Get these two girls out of here," Jenna said in a weak voice, breaking the silence. "We rescued one girl from the van. Her name is Theresa Porchanski. We told her to run away. Someone needs to look for her. And what about the victim in the other bedroom? Is she doing okay?"

There was a slight hesitation before Shane nodded. "Yeah, other than she's pretty out of it. Looks as if she might have been drugged."

"What?" Jenna's eyes filled with horror. Then she grimaced and shook her head. "Oh, no. I can't believe it. We were too late," she whispered.

"That's not true—we saved three of them," Griff reminded her. "And the one who was drugged will recover from this, you'll see."

"Maybe," she said, but her voice was laced with doubt. Griff understood where she was coming from. Some people managed to get hooked on drugs from the very first time they used them.

He could only hope and pray this girl wasn't one of those. That she'd be strong enough to fight back.

But he couldn't risk thinking about the fourth victim now. They had to finish securing the scene, preserving whatever evidence they could. Griff was hopeful that one of the men they'd captured was the elusive Stuart Trent.

And if not, they'd convince one of the others to tell them exactly where to find him.

Two ambulances arrived, one team coming in to where he was waiting with Jenna, the second team heading down the hall to the other victim.

Griff stared down at Jenna, who was looking pale and diaphoretic. Fearing she was headed into shock, he yanked the blanket off the bed and wrapped it around her as best he could while holding pressure to her wound.

"We'll take it from here," one of the paramedics said, gently prying Griff away.

He stumbled backward, giving them the room they needed, then slowly rose to his feet. Griff watched the paramedics fashion a pressure dressing, wishing that he could trade places with Jenna. That he was the one who'd been wounded instead.

"Hang in there, Jenna," he urged. "I'll meet you at the hospital, okay?"

Jenna didn't answer, her expression full of torment and pain.

"Don't worry. She's tough," Declan said as he came up to stand beside Griff. "She'll pull through this."

Griff forced himself to nod, but couldn't help wondering at what cost. He was thankful she was alive but, at the same time, knew that losing the use of her right arm would be detrimental to Jenna's career.

Being a cop was extremely important to her. He suspected Jenna had long defined herself by her choice of career.

How would she handle it if she couldn't continue on the SWAT team? Not very well.

"The deputy chief is on his way," Shane said, coming up to them. "Griff, he's ordered you to stay here until he arrives."

Griff frowned, looking over at Jenna. The paramedics were still working on her wound, but then they would whisk her away to the nearest trauma center. "Too bad. I'm hitching a ride to the hospital with Jenna."

Both Shane and Declan dropped their jaws in identical expressions of shocked surprise. "I must not have heard you correctly," Shane said. "You never disobey a direct order."

Griff couldn't have cared less. His career had already taken a hit—no point in continuing to follow the rules. "Do we have ID's on any of these guys?" he asked, changing the subject. "We're specifically looking for a man named Stuart Trent or a similar alias."

Declan looked down at his notes. "We have a Brian Foogle, Timothy Havlock and James Dunn. Nothing close to Stuart Trent, but maybe he switched up his alias this time."

"Claire," Jenna blurted out as the paramedics bundled her onto the gurney. "You need to find Claire. She'll know if one of these guys is Trent."

"You're right." Griff swung back to Shane and Declan. "Did the local authorities say anything about a sixteen-year-old who looks like Jenna coming in to talk to them?"

His deputies exchanged a blank look. "No, why?"

"We sent her to find help." Griff reached down to take Jenna's uninjured hand, ignoring the way Shane and Declan gaped in surprise at his gesture. "I'm sure she's fine. I'll pick her up and bring her to the hospital, okay?"

Jenna's fingers clung to his for a long second before she let him go. "Thanks."

Griff stepped back, giving the paramedics room to wheel Jenna out to their rig before he turned his attention to Shane and Declan. "Claire has the Dodge. I told her to go to the nearest police station, so I'm assuming she's still there."

"Wait a minute. I thought for sure I saw it

parked a few blocks from here," Shane said with a frown.

A wave of dread washed over him. "Where?" Griff demanded.

"Some corner dive. Gulliver's, I think."

At that moment, his phone signaled an incoming text message. It was Claire asking him to meet her at Gulliver's right away. Griff's heart sank. What if the teen had gone there to search for Shaunee, only to run into Stuart Trent instead?

What if the social-media post was nothing but a trap?

"We have to go, now. Claire just texted me. I think she's in trouble," Griff said in a hoarse voice. If Trent really had Claire, there was no telling what he'd do.

# SEVENTEEN

*No!* Jenna reached out and grabbed the edge of the ambulance door with her left hand in a pathetic attempt to stop the paramedics from taking her away. "Wait," she said weakly. "I want to help Claire. Give me a few minutes."

The paramedic on her left gently pried her fingers off the door frame. "You can't do that. We need to get you to the hospital, right away," he said in a firm tone. The serious expression on his face gave her the sense that the damage to her arm was worse than she'd thought.

"But Claire…" Her voice trailed off. She caught a glimpse of Griff, Shane and Declan all heading out to the squad car at a brisk pace and forced herself to relax.

She could trust Griff. As much as she hated being taken away from the crime scene, she knew that Griff and the rest of the SWAT team would keep working the case until they knew for sure they had Stuart Trent, or whatever name he was using these days, locked up behind bars.

She trusted Griff more than anyone else in the whole world.

The paramedics hovered over her, pumping fluids through her IV and checking her blood pressure, but when they tried to give her something for pain, she refused.

"No, I want to know what's going on," she insisted, attempting to ignore the fact that her right shoulder throbbed painfully. Every so often she glanced down at her right hand, desperately trying to move her wrist or her fingers.

After the third attempt, a wave of panic hit hard, despite her best efforts to control it. What if she lost function in her right arm? What if she couldn't dress herself, much less shoot a gun again?

Her career, her life as she knew it, would be over.

She slammed her eyes shut and took several deep breaths. Playing the what-if game wasn't helpful. She was being whisked away for medical attention. She wasn't a victim; she was strong. Yet a strange sense of doom wouldn't leave her alone, and she desperately needed to know her sister was safe.

Feeling helpless wasn't easy. She was more of a take-charge kind of person. Taking care of others was her forte. Allowing others to take care of her didn't feel right.

She took another deep breath and cleared her mind. Right now, she'd put her future and Claire's in God's hands.

*Dear Lord, please keep Claire, Griff and the rest of the SWAT team safe in Your care. I also ask that You heal my wounds and help me retain the ability to use my right arm, so I can help keep the innocent citizens of Milwaukee safe from harm. Amen.*

The sense of uncontrolled panic eased after she repeated her prayer several times, doing her best to put her faith in God's plan.

When the ambulance arrived at the hospital, the paramedics moved her gurney, sending another shaft of pain spearing deep into her chest. Gritting her teeth, she tried to wait it out, but the paramedic, whose name tag said Ben, had finally had enough.

"You need something for pain," Ben said in a stern tone, as if he were older and in charge, instead of her age. "Let me give you a very small dose, please? We're going to have to move you around, first in the ER and then over to Radiology to get the X-rays you'll need."

The thought of being jostled from one place to another made her moan. "Fine," she agreed. "A small dose. I don't want to be completely knocked out."

"I promise," Ben assured her. "Two milligrams of morphine should help take the edge off."

Jenna watched him put the medication in her intravenous line. She waited for the medication to hit her, but as far as she could tell, the pain level didn't lessen one bit.

When they physically lifted her off the ambulance gurney and onto the ER bed, red dots flashed in front of her eyes as pain swamped her in big, crashing tidal waves. A swarm of hospital personnel buzzed around her, poking and prodding as they examined her. She searched for Dr. Gabby's familiar face among the sea of strangers, but couldn't find it.

Someone tugged at her injured arm and she cried out in pain. A different voice shouted over the din, "Her blood pressure and pulse are too high. Give her some pain meds!"

"Not too much," she tried to protest, but no one paid attention.

In what seemed like a nanosecond, the lights and noise faded away into dark oblivion.

Griff dashed outside the apartment building with Declan and Shane keeping pace behind him. He glanced for a moment at the ambulance carrying Jenna away, then forced himself to focus on the immediate issue at hand.

Skidding to a stop next to the Sheriff's Office

squad car that was parked there, it took him a minute to realize he didn't have the keys.

"Who's driving?" he barked impatiently.

"I am," Declan said, running around to get behind the wheel.

"We need to get over to Gulliver's Grub right away," Griff said, sliding into the passenger seat. He couldn't explain the sense of urgency that nagged at him. The tavern was a public place. There was no logical reason for Claire to be in trouble.

Then again, why was she at Gulliver's Grub at all? Why hadn't she stayed safe at the police station?

Unless she hadn't even made it that far?

A few minutes later Deck pulled into the parking lot of Gulliver's. Bobby's Dodge was the only other vehicle in the lot, and seeing it made Griff's gut twist with fear. He swallowed hard. "Here's the deal. We'll split up. I'm going in the front door, but I need you guys to cover the back."

His deputies exchanged a dark look. "Why don't you let one of us take the front?" Shane suggested.

Griff clenched his jaw, failing to hold back his impatience. "Because Claire knows and trusts me. Let's go."

He quickly climbed out of the car and walked to the front door. He sent up a silent prayer for safety as he waited long enough to make sure Deck and Shane were in place before making a move.

"Ow, you're hurting me," a familiar voice yelled. *Claire?*

"Hurry up. We need to get out of here, now," a male voice said in a nasty tone.

Griff knew he needed to reach Claire immediately. He quickly entered the tavern and, the moment the door closed behind him, found himself staring down the barrel of a gun.

"Stay right where you are, or I'll shoot."

The interior was dimly lit, and an armed man, Stuart Trent most likely, had Claire clamped against his chest in a tight grip. There was a bandage along the right side of his neck, indicating he was the one Claire had stabbed. Fear radiated from Claire's blue eyes although she didn't utter a sound.

"Let her go," Griff said, ignoring the gun barrel pointed at his chest.

The man holding Claire swore as if things weren't going his way. "I expected my boys to help, but I guess I'll have to do this without them."

The place was empty except for a young mixed-race girl who was huddled at the bar, looking pale and afraid. The girl was probably Shaunee, and Griff knew Trent had used

Shaunee's social-media message as bait to get his hands on Claire.

"Let her go, Trent," Griff repeated. "It's over. Your men are in custody and your little enterprise is being shut down for good."

Claire winced as the guy tightened his grip. "Well, well, well. You're a better adversary than I thought. Do you know how many men you've cost me? I shouldn't have tried to get this trouble-maker back, but I wanted her to suffer for stabbing me." Trent's eyes held a mercurial gleam. "I guess it's time for me to start over someplace else." He smirked. "It won't be the first time. And you're going to help me, aren't you?"

"Let her go," Griff repeated.

"No way. She's my ticket out of here, although she's way more trouble than she was worth. Toss your gun on the floor and kick it toward me."

Griff kept his gaze locked on Trent's, but in the periphery he could tell Shane and Deck had come in through the back door. He should have known they wouldn't wait outside. Griff held up his gun and then bent over to place it on the floor. He gave it a slight kick toward Trent, half hoping the guy would be stupid enough to release his grip on Claire long enough to pick it up.

The gun slid to a stop a few feet in front of Trent.

"You want out of here?" Griff said calmly, holding his hands up, palms forward in order to appear less threatening. "Fine with me. Hand over the girl and I'll let you walk away."

"Yeah, right," Trent sneered. He took a few steps forward, dragging Claire along with him. "I'm leaving town and you can be my chauffeur. We'll be long gone before anyone can stop me."

The last thing he wanted to do was get in a car with this guy still holding a gun, but there weren't many options. Deck and Shane couldn't risk taking Trent down without harming Claire.

"No!" Shaunee suddenly shouted, as if someone had poked her with a hot stick. She dropped to the floor, picked up Griff's gun and began waving it around. "You can't leave me," she begged, her eyes wild. "I need you! I'll shoot. I swear I'll shoot all of you!"

The girl's irrational rant caught Trent off guard, and he loosened his hold on Claire, ducking as Shaunee turned the gun in his direction.

Deck and Shane made the most of his momentary lapse, grabbing him from behind and wrestling the gun out of his grip.

"Calm down," Griff said to Shaunee, who was openly crying now. "It's okay. We'll help you. You're safe now."

Shaunee crumpled and he just managed to grab the gun from her trembling hand before she collapsed onto the floor. The girl was falling apart and Griff believed her drug addiction was a contributing factor.

"Leave me alone," Shaunee whimpered, shrinking from his touch.

He stood and backed away, giving her the space she wanted. The girl was in bad shape, needing medical attention, so he quickly called for another ambulance.

As he finished the call, Claire ran toward him, throwing herself into his arms. "You came," she sobbed brokenly. "You came for me."

"Of course," he answered gruffly, patting her awkwardly on the back.

"I'm sorry. I shouldn't have tried to find Shaunee on my own. Where's Jenna?" Claire lifted her head, glancing around with a frown. "Why isn't she here with you?"

Griff tightened his grip on her. "She was hit in the shoulder and is on her way to the hospital," he said.

Claire's eyes filled with tears. "Will you take me to see her?"

"Go ahead," Declan said. "We'll finish things up here."

Leaving was the last thing he should do. His boss would be here any moment, and there would be endless interviews and reams of paperwork to fill out, in order to explain what had transpired.

Yet none of that seemed to matter at the moment. Allowing Jenna to be taken away without him at her side had been difficult. He wasn't going to leave her alone for a second longer.

She needed his support, whether she admitted it or not.

And maybe he needed her, too.

"Thanks," he said to Deck, putting his arm around Claire's shoulders. "Tell Markham that I'll get in touch soon. Oh, and you better tell the FBI to arrest attorney Darnell Franklin. He's a key part of this trafficking ring."

Shane's jaw dropped open in shock when Griff turned to leave, but Deck simply grinned. "Will do."

This time, walking away was easy. Griff ushered Claire back out to the Dodge, knowing that following his heart was the right thing to do.

God would want him to forgive Helen for whatever role she'd played in the re-adoption scam. And it occurred to him that Jenna was right. God had forgiven him, too. Because the guilt that was once so heavy on his shoulders seemed to have lightened.

Because of Jenna. She'd shown him so much, not just what a true partnership could be, but the value of faith.

He loved her. More than he'd thought possible. More than he'd loved Helen.

Of course, Jenna might not feel the same way,

but he was determined to give her all the time she needed.

He refused to let her go without a fight.

Jenna slowly regained consciousness, confused about where she was. The weird beeping noises and antiseptic smell made her realize she was in the hospital.

The details of her injury came rushing forward, and she turned her head, looking down at her bandaged right arm. Her hand and fingers were swollen, and when she tried to wiggle them there was no movement.

She squeezed her eyes shut, trying not to panic. What would she do if her career was over? What could she do with only one hand?

How would she support herself and Claire?

And what about Griff? She couldn't bear to see the pity in his eyes once he learned the truth. For years she'd kept her childhood abuse a secret because she didn't want anyone feeling sorry for her. Now here she was again, in another situation that would only garner pity.

No, she couldn't do it. Griff deserved someone better. She'd need to stay away, hiding her true feelings for him.

She refused to be some sort of charity case.

A knock on her door made her want to scream *go away*, but she swallowed the words before they could erupt from her throat. But she couldn't seem to push words past her frozen vocal cords, either, to invite them in.

The person on the other side of the door pushed it open a crack to peer in. Griff. For some odd reason the sight of him made her want to cry.

"May we come in?" he asked hesitantly.

We? Knowing that he must have found Claire brought a wave of relief. "Sure," she croaked in a hoarse voice.

He pushed the door open and came in, with Claire right behind him. "Hey, Jenna, how are you feeling?" Claire asked, her gaze full of concern.

"Like I was hit by a cement truck," she said, striving for a light tone. "I'm glad you're safe, Claire."

"Griff saved me," her sister said. "And the guys from the SWAT team arrested Stuart Trent, and they're going to find and arrest Darnell Franklin, too."

"What?" Jenna felt as if her mind was nothing but Swiss cheese. "I don't understand."

"Claire went to find Shaunee, but stumbled over Trent instead," Griff said. "He used Shaunee as bait and was planning to leave with Claire when we showed up." He frowned. "In fact, Trent made it sound like he'd done something similar before."

"Shaunee came through, in the end," Claire defended the other girl.

Jenna could tell Griff didn't necessarily agree. "So it's over. We shut down the trafficking ring."

"Yeah, we did," Griff agreed.

"But we still need to find the rest of the girls," Claire pointed out.

"We will," he assured her.

Jenna let out a heavy breath. The nightmare was over. Time to go their separate ways, especially considering the extent of her injury.

A career-ending, life-changing injury.

"Will you let Claire hang out with you until I'm discharged from the hospital?" she asked.

"Of course," Griff answered readily. "In fact, I'll have to rent a house until the damage to my place has been repaired."

Jenna avoided his direct gaze. "I guess you can see I'll be out on medical leave indefinitely. So I just wanted to say thanks. Thanks for everything." She added a note of finality to her tone, hoping Griff understood their time together was over.

He scowled. "I'm going to stay with you to see this through, Jenna, no matter what."

She shook her head. "Don't," she pleaded. "I'm not interested."

"I don't believe you," Griff said in a low tone, stepping forward to take hold of her left hand. "I understand you're scared, but we'll get through this together."

"There is no together," she said, trying not to

cling to his hand. She was all too aware of Claire watching them, as if trying to understand what was going on.

"Jenna, I—" He was interrupted by a doctor walking unannounced into her room.

"Good morning," he greeted Jenna. "How's your arm?"

Even though she didn't really want to discuss the massive extent of her injury in front of Griff, she knew he probably needed to hear every last detail. So he could understand why there wasn't a future for them.

Personally or professionally.

She refused to be a victim. She'd find some way to make a living, but without Griff. Someday he'd thank her for forcing them to go their separate ways.

"I can't feel anything or move my wrist or my fingers," she said bluntly. "The bullet must have severed a nerve."

"No, there wasn't any nerve damage, but we did use a nerve block during surgery. The numbness will wear off soon, so you'll want to take some pain meds before it goes away completely."

Nerve block? Her heart filled with hope. "So I'll be able to use my arm again?"

"Absolutely. The muscle damage wasn't as bad as we'd feared, although certainly it'll take time to heal. But with good rehab and physical therapy, you should be able to get a hundred percent of your function back."

"Really?" She was afraid to hope. "Then why couldn't I use my hand right after I was shot?"

"Shock," the surgeon said confidently. "We tested your nerve function prior to the nerve block, so I know there wasn't any permanent damage." He paused, then added, "We'll be back later to change your dressing."

He left, but she barely noticed. No permanent damage. Jenna couldn't believe what she was hearing. No permanent damage! She silently offered up a prayer of thanks.

"You're going to be all right, aren't you, Jenna?" Claire asked, seeking reassurance.

"I guess I am," Jenna murmured. Still, she tried once again to pull her hand from Griff's.

"Claire, would you give us a moment alone?" he asked.

"Uh, sure. Yeah. No problem." Claire ducked out the door before Jenna could ask her to stay.

"Listen, Griff," she began, but he shook his head.

"I know what you were trying to do, but it's not going to be that easy to get rid of me. Injured arm or not, I'm not leaving. I love you, Jenna," he said, taking her completely by surprise. "I know it's too soon for you, and that you deserve someone better, but I need you. I don't want to think about what my life will be like without you."

She stared at him, at a loss for words. Never had any man made such a heartfelt declaration to her. "I care about you, too, Griff. But my life is complicated right now. Between the injury and finding a way to get custody of Claire…"

"We'll work everything out, together."

She wished it was as simple as it sounded. "Claire's going to have rough times ahead, and it won't be easy. She's a teenager and we've already seen her attitude firsthand. Why would you want to hang around for more?"

His fingers tightened around hers. "I always wanted a big family," he said in a low tone. "The night Helen was killed we were fighting over the fact that I wanted us to start a family, but she wasn't interested."

Her heart went out to him all over again. "I'm sorry," she whispered.

He flashed a crooked smile. "God's plan, remember? Besides, I've come to realize how the two of us together make a great team."

"Together," Jenna whispered. "I like the sound of that."

"Me, too." Griff leaned over and pressed a kiss to her cheek. "I've been alone for so long, I forgot what it was like to have a true partner. You've made me realize what I've missed. Not just sharing a life together, but being connected to someone emotionally, too. Now that I've found you, I'm never going to let you go."

Humbled, Jenna could only stare at him. "Oh, Griff," she finally managed. "I've tried to hold back, to keep things professional between us, but I failed miserably. You should know I've fallen in love with you, too."

"Really?" His eyes lit up with hope and happiness. "That's not the effects of anesthesia talking, is it?"

She chuckled, then winced as a tingling sensation danced down her injured arm. "No, it's not. I love you," she repeated. "I'll transfer to a different SWAT team if that's what it takes to be with you."

"Since I just promoted Caleb to sergeant, you can report to him, instead of me. Trust me, everything will work out fine."

Ironically, she did trust Griff. Despite her past experiences with men.

She trusted him with her life and with her heart.

"Yay!" Claire crowed, entering the room enthusiastically. "I knew things would work out between you two. I just knew it!"

Jenna smiled when Griff reached out to draw Claire close to her bedside, knowing she was truly blessed.

# EPILOGUE

Griff shuffled his feet nervously as he stood outside Jenna's front door. The past three months had been grueling; regaining the full use of her arm was more time-consuming than they'd expected.

But today Jenna had been authorized to go back to work, and he'd been offered the promotion to replace Deputy Chief Markham when he retired at the end of the month. Everything was falling into place.

Wrapping his fingers around the ring box, he tried to quell a sudden attack of the jitters. They'd taken things slow, partially because of Jenna's injury and partially because of the red tape they'd had to slice through for Jenna to be granted custody of Claire. Jenna and Claire had gone together to visit their mother in jail, and Georgina Towne had confirmed what they'd already suspected, that at five years old, Jenna had been taken away from her mother due to her substance abuse and neglect. Her parental rights had been terminated and Jenna had been given up for adoption—a legal one through the state, like Claire's initial adoption by the Bronsons.

Jenna had taken the news in stride, even though she'd never understand why her adopted mother hadn't told her the truth.

Griff grasped the ring again and took a deep breath. No reason to think Jenna might have changed her mind about their relationship.

Claire was celebrating with friends tonight as a treat for passing her final exams. He knew she kept in touch with Shaunee, who'd been released from rehab. He was proud of the way they were both turning their lives around.

No more stalling. Griff lifted his hand and rapped on the door. He could hear footsteps before Jenna opened it.

She looked beautiful, wearing a blue knit dress that matched her eyes and left her arms bare. Her surgical scar had grown less noticeable over time. And she'd left her long hair down, the way he liked it. "Hi," he managed. "You look amazing."

Jenna blushed. "Thanks." Griff held out his hand, wrapping his fingers gently around hers.

They walked down the street to where he'd left his car, and when he opened the passenger door for her she let out a laugh.

"What's so funny?" he asked as she slid into the seat.

"Remember how I yelled at you that first night when you opened the door for me?" she asked.

"I'm not likely to forget," Griff said drily. He closed the door behind her, then went around to climb into the driver's seat.

She reached out to touch his arm. "When I'm with you, being treated like a woman doesn't make me feel weak, but strong."

"You're the strongest woman I know," he said honestly. "You never complained about the endless therapy sessions, either."

She shrugged. "Complaining was useless. I was on a mission to get better. Where are we going?"

"Antonio's," he answered, hiding a grin when she widened her eyes.

"Pricey," she murmured.

It was a special occasion, but she didn't know that yet. "A friend was raving about it. Figured we should give it a try."

"Okay." She settled back in her seat.

The drive didn't take long, and she brought him up to date on Claire's progress. "She'll have one more year of high school to complete, but she seems okay with that."

"I'm glad. She's already had to grow up too fast." Griff parked and went around to open Jenna's door. He palmed the ring box in his left hand and subtly passed it to the maître d', who tucked it out of sight.

They were provided a quiet table in the corner as he'd requested. Jenna nibbled her lip as she perused the menu, obviously worrying too much about the prices.

"Relax," he said. "I received some great news today."

Her eyes widened. "You were offered the job!" she exclaimed, leaping out of her seat and coming around to hug him. "Oh, Griff, I'm so happy for you!"

"Me, too," he said, crushing her close. "But it's not the salary I care about as much as making sure we run a tight, clean department. I care about upholding the law. I don't want any dirty cops on my watch."

She brushed a quick kiss over his mouth, then returned to her seat. "Helen's sins aren't yours," she reminded him.

He knew that, although after Franklin's arrest it became clear that Helen had in fact participated in the illegal re-adoptions. On at least two occasions, her name was clearly listed on re-adoption paperwork as the attorney of record. As a lawyer, she should have known better, but he was willing to give her the benefit of the doubt.

The DNA from Jenna's hand wound had also proved that the man who shot Jenna at the apartment building was the same one who'd attacked her outside her home.

At least Jenna's father was no longer a threat. It hadn't taken him long to try to steal liquor, which landed him back in jail to serve out the rest of his sentence.

Jenna ordered a steak and a salad, and he did the same. When the salads were brought out in covered dishes, she frowned, puzzled.

"What's this, a secret salad?" When she lifted the top and found a small ring box sitting on a plate, with no salad in sight, she gaped in surprise. Then her gaze met his. "Griff?"

He came over to bend down on one knee beside her chair. "Jenna, will you please marry me?"

"Oh, Griff. Yes. Yes, I'll marry you." She didn't even touch the ring box, leaning over to kiss him instead. "I love you," she whispered.

"I love you, too." He knew he couldn't have made a better choice in a partner, wife and future mother of their children.

A future truly worth celebrating.

\* \* \* \* \*

Dear Reader,

I'm humbled and awed at the wonderful letters, emails and Facebook messages you've sent about how much you're enjoying my SWAT: Top Cops—Love in the Line of Duty series. It's amazing how you've come to care about these wonderful characters as much as I do.

*Mirror Image* is the sixth and final book in the series. I knew from the moment I introduced Griff Vaughn that he needed his own story, and who better to pair him with than the tough, edgy sharpshooter Jenna Reed? After Griff tragically loses his young wife, he wrestles with guilt over the role he played in the car crash on that fateful night. He's determined to live alone, dedicating his life to his career, until Jenna becomes the target of a vicious attack.

Jenna hasn't had good experiences with men and figures Griff is no exception—until she realizes what a great team they make, in fighting danger and in matters of the heart.

I hope you enjoyed Griff and Jenna's story.

I love hearing from my readers. Drop by my website at www.laurascottbooks.com to either leave me a brief note or sign up for my newsletter. I'm also on Facebook at Laura Scott Books Author and on Twitter: @Laurascottbooks.

Yours in faith,

*Laura Scott*

# LARGER-PRINT BOOKS!

## GET 2 FREE
## LARGER-PRINT NOVELS
## PLUS 2 FREE
## MYSTERY GIFTS

*Love Inspired*®
# SUSPENSE
RIVETING INSPIRATIONAL ROMANCE

### *Larger-print novels are now available...*

# LARGER-PRINT BOOKS!

## GET 2 FREE LARGER-PRINT NOVELS PLUS 2 FREE MYSTERY GIFTS

*Love Inspired*®

### Larger-print novels are now available...

**YES!** Please send me 2 FREE LARGER-PRINT Love Inspired® novels and my 2 FREE mystery gifts (gifts are worth about $10). After receiving them, if I don't wish to receive any more books, I can return the shipping statement marked "cancel." If I don't cancel, I will receive 6 brand-new novels every month and be billed just $5.49 per book in the U.S. or $5.99 per book in Canada. That's a savings of at least 19% off the cover price. It's quite a bargain! Shipping and handling is just 50¢ per book in the U.S. and 75¢ per book in Canada.* I understand that accepting the 2 free books and gifts places me under no obligation to buy anything. I can always return a shipment and cancel at any time. Even if I never buy another book, the two free books and gifts are mine to keep forever.

122/322 IDN GH6D

Name _____ (PLEASE PRINT)

Address _____ Apt. #

City _____ State/Prov. _____ Zip/Postal Code

Signature (if under 18, a parent or guardian must sign)

### Mail to the Reader Service:
**IN U.S.A.:** P.O. Box 1867, Buffalo, NY 14240-1867
**IN CANADA:** P.O. Box 609, Fort Erie, Ontario L2A 5X3

**Are you a current subscriber to Love Inspired® books and want to receive the larger-print edition?**
**Call 1-800-873-8635 or visit www.ReaderService.com.**

* Terms and prices subject to change without notice. Prices do not include applicable taxes. Sales tax applicable in N.Y. Canadian residents will be charged applicable taxes. Offer not valid in Quebec. This offer is limited to one order per household. Not valid to current subscribers to Love Inspired Larger-Print books. All orders subject to credit approval. Credit or debit balances in a customer's account(s) may be offset by any other outstanding balance owed by or to the customer. Please allow 4 to 6 weeks for delivery. Offer available while quantities last.

**Your Privacy**—The Reader Service is committed to protecting your privacy. Our Privacy Policy is available online at www.ReaderService.com or upon request from the Reader Service.

We make a portion of our mailing list available to reputable third parties that offer products we believe may interest you. If you prefer that we not exchange your name with third parties, or if you wish to clarify or modify your communication preferences, please visit us at www.ReaderService.com/consumerschoice or write to us at Reader Service Preference Service, P.O. Box 9062, Buffalo, NY 14240-9062. Include your complete name and address.

LILP15

# REQUEST YOUR FREE BOOKS!
## 2 FREE WHOLESOME ROMANCE NOVELS
## IN LARGER PRINT
## PLUS 2
# FREE
## MYSTERY GIFTS

༺ ༻ ༺ ༻ ༺ ༻ ༺ ༻ ༺ ༻ ༺ ༻ ༺ ༻ ༺ ༻ ༺ ༻

## HEARTWARMING™

ༀ ༀ ༀ ༀ ༀ ༀ ༀ ༀ ༀ ༀ ༀ ༀ ༀ ༀ ༀ ༀ

*Wholesome, tender romances*

---

**YES!** Please send me 2 FREE Harlequin® Heartwarming Larger-Print novels and my 2 FREE mystery gifts (gifts worth about $10). After receiving them, if I don't wish to receive any more books, I can return the shipping statement marked "cancel." If I don't cancel, I will receive 4 brand-new larger-print novels every month and be billed just $5.24 per book in the U.S. or $5.99 per book in Canada. That's a savings of at least 19% off the cover price. It's quite a bargain! Shipping and handling is just 50¢ per book in the U.S. and 75¢ per book in Canada.* I understand that accepting the 2 free books and gifts places me under no obligation to buy anything. I can always return a shipment and cancel at any time. Even if I never buy another book, the two free books and gifts are mine to keep forever.

161/361 IDN GHX2

| | |
|---|---|
| Name | (PLEASE PRINT) |

| | | |
|---|---|---|
| Address | | Apt. # |

| | | |
|---|---|---|
| City | State/Prov. | Zip/Postal Code |

Signature (if under 18, a parent or guardian must sign)

### Mail to the **Reader Service:**
**IN U.S.A.:** P.O. Box 1867, Buffalo, NY 14240-1867
**IN CANADA:** P.O. Box 609, Fort Erie, Ontario L2A 5X3

* Terms and prices subject to change without notice. Prices do not include applicable taxes. Sales tax applicable in N.Y. Canadian residents will be charged applicable taxes. Offer not valid in Quebec. This offer is limited to one order per household. Not valid for current subscribers to Harlequin Heartwarming larger-print books. All orders subject to credit approval. Credit or debit balances in a customer's account(s) may be offset by any other outstanding balance owed by or to the customer. Please allow 4 to 6 weeks for delivery. Offer available while quantities last.

---

**Your Privacy**—The Reader Service is committed to protecting your privacy. Our Privacy Policy is available online at www.ReaderService.com or upon request from the Reader Service.

We make a portion of our mailing list available to reputable third parties that offer products we believe may interest you. If you prefer that we not exchange your name with third parties, or if you wish to clarify or modify your communication preferences, please visit us at www.ReaderService.com/consumerschoice or write to us at Reader Service Preference Service, P.O. Box 9062, Buffalo, NY 14240-9062. Include your complete name and address.

HW15

MONTANA MAVERICKS

**YES!** Please send me **The Montana Mavericks Collection** in Larger Print. This collection begins with 3 FREE books and 2 FREE gifts (gifts valued at approx. $20.00 retail) in the first shipment, along with the other first 4 books from the collection! If I do not cancel, I will receive 8 monthly shipments until I have the entire 51-book Montana Mavericks collection. I will receive 2 or 3 FREE books in each shipment and I will pay just $4.99 US/ $5.89 CDN for each of the other four books in each shipment, plus $2.99 for shipping and handling per shipment.*If I decide to keep the entire collection, I'll have paid for only 32 books, because 19 books are FREE! I understand that accepting the 3 free books and gifts places me under no obligation to buy anything. I can always return a shipment and cancel at any time. My free books and gifts are mine to keep no matter what I decide.

263 HCN 2404   463 HCN 2404

Name _____ (PLEASE PRINT)

Address _____ Apt. #

City _____ State/Prov. _____ Zip/Postal Code

Signature (if under 18, a parent or guardian must sign)

### Mail to the **Reader Service:**
**IN U.S.A.:** P.O. Box 1867, Buffalo, NY 14240-1867
**IN CANADA:** P.O. Box 609, Fort Erie, Ontario L2A 5X3

# READERSERVICE.COM

## Manage your account online!

- Review your order history
- Manage your payments
- Update your address

> *We've designed the*
> *Reader Service website*
> *just for you.*

## Enjoy all the features!

- Discover new series available to you, and read excerpts from any series.
- Respond to mailings and special monthly offers.
- Connect with favorite authors at the blog.
- Browse the Bonus Bucks catalog and online-only exclusives.
- Share your feedback.

*Visit us at:*
# ReaderService.com